# Breakpoints

## Wayne
## Dean-Richards

'No story is complete without its past.' – Peter Straub

'We are the sum of what we lack' – Alan Rickman

Published by
SPOUTING FORTH INK
Thimblemill Library
Thimblemill Road
Smethwick
Sandwell
West Midlands
B67 5RJ

ISBN – 0 9531 472 5 8

British Library Cataloguing-in-publication Data.
A catalogue record for this book is available from the British Library.

Published with the financial support of West Midlands Arts

## About the author

Wayne Dean-Richards has been, amongst other things, an industrial cleaner, an actor, a boxer, a caretaker, a lecturer and a teacher. His stories and poems have been published in the UK and the US, in magazines and anthologies. His poetry collections are: *Poems By Two Fat Men, Clinging To The Wreckage* and *Thicker Than Water*. A number of his stories are collected in *At The Edge* – together with poems by Geoff Stevens. He is an acclaimed reader of his work.

# ONE

This is what happened:

December 17<sup>th</sup>. Neck aching from looking out of the window for so long, D.S. Charlie Grant narrowed his eyes against the lights from Churchill House, one of six multi-storey flats at the heart of the Beeches Farm Estate. It was almost midnight. Cold. No moon. Charlie Grant passed his tongue over his teeth. Nights, especially winter, with its bright lights, litter, and noise, the Estate was like a funfair - minus the fun.

Charlie eyed his new partner. D.S. Tony Harris held himself very still. Harris was twenty-six. Acted younger but looked older. Charlie could see, despite the cold, his partner was sweating. He said:

"How're you doing?"

D.S. Harris tossed two more Tunes into his mouth. Already he was on his third pack, and the car reeked of menthol.

"Good," Harris replied.

That wasn't how he looked, but Charlie decided not to push it, to go over the details again instead:

"Leroy says when the man buzzes him on the intercom, he'll turn on his kitchen light. Our man's got to go in, get up to the ninth floor, and knock on Leroy's door. We follow him in, watch the transaction - make the arrest."

Charlie waited for a reaction. But Harris just sucked Tunes and glanced at his watch. It'd been like that all night. Harris was suffering. Charlie saw it and considered going inside - waiting there, but dismissed the idea: If they went inside, they'd draw attention. Besides which: inside or outside, waiting was still top of the agenda: if they waited inside instead of outside, it wouldn't be any easier on Harris.

He saw his partner was losing control, becoming a mass of tics. Setting something in motion then waiting for it to happen, hoping it would - at the same time dreading it – wasn't so much a talent as an aptitude. This was the second time he'd been out with him, and Charlie was starting to think it was something his partner wasn't cut out for. He watched Tony Harris twist the wrappers of the two Tunes he'd just popped into his mouth. His eyes were on his partner for just a few seconds. But when he looked up at Churchill House, the light in Leroy's kitchen was on.

"Shit!"

When D.S. Harris reached the Main Entrance to Churchill House, he was breathing hard. Wincing at the smell of disinfectant, he followed D.S. Grant across the lobby to the lift, the sound of their shoes on the tile floor ricocheting off the low tin ceiling.

The lift was directly opposite the Main Entrance. It was already in use. Knowing if they were to witness the transaction they had only a couple of minutes to get up there, Harris thumbed the call button.

Seeing it was useless, Charlie said:

"We'll take the stairs."

Gulping in air, Charlie took the stairs the way his new partner ate Tunes: quickly. Harris followed suit, but was soon labouring.

"You go on," Harris gasped as they reached the fourth floor.

Charlie saw his partner was all in - his face red, his mouth opening and closing like the gills of a dying fish. What should he do? The stink of disinfectant was overlaid by the stink of dog shit, the shit all over the stairs: shit icing on a concrete cake, making it hard to think straight.

"I'll wait for the lift," Harris panted.

When his partner spoke, Charlie saw his tongue was coated with menthol. He hesitated, gripping the steel handrail so tightly the blood drained from his knuckles.

"Go on," Harris urged, dabbing at the sweat on his forehead with the sleeve of his jacket.

"When I get there I won't make any sudden moves. Even so, if he sees me our man'll run. He won't be able to get to the stairs - I'll be in his way. So he'll go for the lift. When you step out of the lift, we'll talk to him, and if we're lucky he won't do anything stupid. Okay?"

Harris nodded, again dabbing at his forehead with his sleeve.

When he reached the sixth floor, Charlie heard the lift, grinding upwards, and pushed himself harder, lactic acid burning in his thighs.

It wasn't the way it'd been on the ground floor: this time when Harris thumbed the call button, the lift arrived immediately. Before his shift he'd eaten tikka masala with pilau rice. Since then he'd put away three packets of Tunes. Harris was used to indigestion, but this felt like hot fingers tearing at his gut. Even though he'd stopped running, his heart was beating too fast, his fear in the driving seat. When the door screeched open, Harris brought his hands up to protect his face...but the lift contained only a pool of piss shaped like Australia.

2

Harris stepped past it and pressed 9. He was glad Grant wasn't there to see his fear. His tongue was so dry he feared it'd crack. He wished he had more Tunes or, better still, a cool drink. Or better still: that he was home with Allison. She'd be in bed by now. Would have on the portable TV. Would probably be watching the Sherlock Holmes movie, Basil Rathbone as Holmes, though she'd be too worried about him to enjoy it. Tony Harris liked the fact that his wife worried about him. What he didn't like was: with this kind of gig, she had cause to.

The lift door scraped open. Harris wanted to run, but his ambition held him in place. "So," he mouthed, and dry-swallowed before stepping out onto the ninth floor.

The lights had all been gouged out. Blinking, Harris waited for his eyes to adjust to the near-darkness. Then he stepped into the middle of the corridor and looked left and right, like a boy about to cross a busy road. Seeing light spilling from the open door of one of the flats, Harris convinced himself this was Leroy Blackstock's place. Grant had said to wait, he knew that, but he was here to get himself noticed, and one way of getting noticed was to go it alone, get this thing done.

Breathing soundlessly, Harris edged towards the light...

Close to Leroy's apartment now, Harris heard voices. He saw two men: a tall man, framed by the doorway, wearing a hooded top and dungarees; and a man standing directly in front of him, not as tall, but more solidly built, wearing a leather jacket and baggy jeans.

Harris saw himself accepting a commendation, becoming a D.I., Allison - newly kitted out in a dark green dress - watching him, listening to his acceptance speech: under-played, so he seemed modest.

Close, now, the men's voices were booming in his ears - though he still couldn't make out what they were saying, the walls fracturing their words - Harris reached for his I.D. just as the stockier of the men, alerted to his presence by Leroy's gaze, turned, and saw him.

What he'd do, Harris, decided, was make sure in his speech he squeezed in the word 'duty'. That always went down well.

"Police-" D.S. Harris said...He didn't get to finish his sentence.

His thighs burning, Charlie Grant stepped onto the ninth floor at the moment Leroy slammed shut the door to his flat, plunging the corridor into darkness. Charlie groped towards the sound, knowing he mustn't rush, fighting to steady his breathing. His stomach was tense, the muscles hard. Someone was close - Charlie sensed it. Adrenalin pumped through him and his left wrist started to hurt, a clear, sharp pain, as if it'd just been broken. In fact it'd been twenty years since that

3

break, but it was a mistake to think you could outdistance your past - the best you could hope for was to find some way to deal with it.

Charlie made out a sloth-like shape on the floor outside Leroy's flat: Tony Harris, down, hurt - he didn't know how badly. If you were inexperienced - or lacked the ability to stay calm, in control of your actions - and you saw your partner on the floor, you ran towards him, forgetting everything else. Let yourself do that and you'd made a mistake - one that could cost you. Charlie hated violence. It sickened him. But that didn't alter the fact that he was a man who could stay calm when violence was so close he felt its hot breath on his face. Now, instead of rushing to help his partner, Charlie stood still, certain someone was waiting in the darkness. Keeping his voice low, he said:

"Run."

For three or four seconds, there was no movement or sound. Then Charlie heard footsteps, going away from him. A moment later, he heard the lift door scrape open, and knew he was able at last to kneel down and find out if Tony Harris was alive or dead.

# TWO

C.I. Dennis Grant, an inch taller and twenty-five pounds heavier than his older brother Charlie, his smile fixed in place, acutely aware of the positive effect of his immaculate dinner suit, placed his fists on the table before him and stood to face the brass. It was almost midnight, and most of the faces directed at him were the worse for wear - cheeks reddened by booze, eyes made watery by cigar smoke. Dennis Grant passed his smile around, then began his speech:

"We don't often get this many senior police officers in Benbury, and I do appreciate the fact that some of you have driven a long way to be here, which is why I made it clear: nothing within two miles of the Convention Centre was to be ticketed!"

The laughter sounded like cold water poured onto a hot pan, and Dennis Grant's smile became real, for he knew he had his audience in the palm of his hand. He planned in two more years – tops - to be heading a regional crime squad, having left Benbury, maybe the Midlands altogether; this evening formed part of that plan.

Rachel Grant, in a black suede button through dress, reached for her orange juice, misjudged the distance between her hand and the glass, and knocked it over, this constituting living, breathing irony since she was the only wholly sober guest at the Convention Centre.

Dennis Grant's smile didn't falter though he was pissed off at Rachel. The bitch wanted to see him fail, the same as everyone, Dennis was convinced of it, but he was determined not to fail! With barely a pause, he continued.

Who the hell did Dennis think he was kidding? Rachel wondered, righting her glass and dabbing at the spilled juice with a napkin, certain he wanted to let go his smile and stab her with a disapproving look.

Rachel crumpled the wet napkin. Getting ready for this evening, noting his scrutiny of her she'd said: "What you'd really like is a robot. Something that looks perfect, smiles in all the right places, says nothing. Something you plug in. Something you don't have to give anything back to. Like in *The Stepford Wives*." As usual, Dennis hadn't replied. The part of her husband's body Rachel was most intimate with, was his back. That wasn't a good thing. It occurred to her that if she stood, right now, and called him an arse-kisser, she'd get his attention.

*Hey, arse-kisser!*

5

Then Dennis wouldn't be able to hold onto his smile, and the Commissioner's face would get even redder. The Commissioner was Dennis' hero, a master of fast track who attended church on Sunday, put serious time into polishing the brass buttons on his dress uniform, called his wife: 'My angel', though Rachel'd felt his eyes sliding over her breasts and her hips, making her skin crawl.

*Hey, arse-kisser!*

She'd love to do it, but knew she couldn't. So what were her alternatives? She glanced over at the Commissioner's wife. The 'angel' sat waxwork-still, the gold chains around her neck bringing to mind a photograph of the Olympic swimmer Mark Spitz. What were the angel's medals a reward for? For being the wife of a careerist - for sitting very still and never answering back?

So suddenly the movement jolted the muscles at the side of her neck,
Rachel turned away from the Commissioner's wife. At thirty-two, you knew yourself a little if you were lucky. (Or unlucky, depending on what you knew.) Rachel knew becoming a version of the Commissioner's wife, posed and poised and dead inside - wasn't an alternative.

In Benbury drug-related crime and violent crime in general was on the increase. But in Benbury traffic offences great and small were prosecuted with vigour.

C.I. Dennis Grant said:

"There's been a two per-cent increase in prosecution in the past three months. Consistent with this is the emphasis I've placed on competition. Competitiveness is a good thing - it breeds commitment, it makes officers work hard. My officers know if they work hard, they'll be rewarded. Early in the New Year one D.S. will be promoted to D.I. There'll be no more promotions till June. My officers know if they want to progress, they've got to be productive, so they pull out all the stops: competition breeds commitment!"

Rachel had already sat through the speech a dozen times, and felt now as if she were drowning in it. She tried to breathe deeply. But the air was warm and smoky. Dennis pressed on, the brass and their wives sat drinking, waitresses in white blouses moved with tired grace among the circular tables. Rachel's throat tightened. She gripped the edge of the table. Felt her head start to spin. Any time she got tired of one way traffic and tried to speak to him, Dennis cut her off, snapping: "You want me to fail." Rachel denied it: "I don't want you to fail. I just don't want your career, you getting what you want, to be the only thing that counts, I want…" Which he took as a cue: "I want!" he'd repeat, and turn up the volume on the TV: end of conversation. Already this was a ritual, which

6

realisation took Rachel back to her alternatives. Should she stand and shout? No - she couldn't do it. Should she die and be embalmed in gold, like the Commissioner's wife? No - she couldn't do that either. So what then?

From the corner of his eye Dennis saw Rachel push back her chair. Stand up. Her walking out in the middle of his speech didn't look good, he knew, and was tempted to put his hand on her shoulder and push her back down onto her seat, point his finger at her, tell her to stay put. In his estimation the brass would approve of a senior officer showing he didn't take any shit, not even from his wife, but they wouldn't be able to admit it: they'd have to act as if they disapproved. So Dennis decided to ignore her departure, to keep going, smooth, first smiling again - then frowning to make sure everyone saw how serious he was: a man who was going places.

Dennis machine-gunned his audience with a series of statistics as Rachel left. He held up his right hand and counted off recent improvements, careful not to claim full credit, leaving that to his audience.

"What the C.I.D. needs, is vision," Dennis said. Time was he'd have been able to say it plain, say: 'men of vision.' Not that, when you got right down to it, it really mattered. The people here did know what he *really* meant. Dennis used his fingers to wipe away his frown, then put his smile back on.

"Are you alright, love?"

This from one of the waitresses: Mid-twenties, dark hair piled high.

Being called 'love' was one of Rachel's pet hates, but she saw the woman meant well, so she let it go, saying:

"I'm fine, thanks." The old lie.

Stepping past the waitress, Rachel walked quickly away from the Function Room. Out here, the air was cooler, yet the corridor was so narrow she felt little better. She needed to get outside, but each corridor fed into another that looked identical to it. At first she smiled, wishing she'd carried a slice of bread from the Function Room so she could lay a trail of crumbs, like Hansel and Gretel, but after fifteen minutes her anxiety was building and her smile had vanished.

Two hours later Rachel was still tense, still slightly breathless, as if, no matter how hard she tried, she couldn't fill her lungs.

She crossed to Dennis' side of the bedroom.

"You were very good tonight," she said, putting her arms around his waist. Conceived to impress the brass, Rachel was sure his speech and how he delivered it had done just that. Holding herself tight against him, she closed her eyes.

7

Dennis was a big man. She liked his solidity, had always drawn some comfort from it. Things could be worked out. Towards which end it was essential they make love. Most nights, when Dennis finally got home from work, his face had the slack, pouchy look of an old man. Thinking of it, they hadn't made love since she'd talked about having a baby at the start of autumn. Rachel opened her eyes. Moved back to her dresser. Took the case in which she kept her diaphragm from her jewellery box and opened it so Dennis could see it was empty.

They *had* to make love! Only when they'd really made love, emptying themselves, would they be able to talk. She'd tell Dennis she wasn't against him, didn't want him to fail...only she couldn't be like the Commissioner's wife.

The muscles in Dennis Grant's neck tightened. He judged from the look on her face that the bitch wasn't satisfied with trying to foul up his speech, had something else planned - walking out had been the main course, now dessert was on its way.

Rachel wanted to have Dennis make some space to listen instead of showing her his back all the time. All this had to be said. But first...first they had to make love. She reached to touch his face, wanting things to work out, wanting that more than anything.

But before she could touch him, Dennis grabbed her wrist, his grip so tight it hurt.

"Dennis!"

"Get this straight," he said, squeezing her wrist, seeing how the pressure of his fingers discoloured her flesh. "I don't need you." He squeezed harder. "Not tonight, not ever," he said. Then he let go, presenting her resolutely, irrevocably with his back.

# THREE

December 18<sup>th</sup>.

"Open up, Leroy. This is D.S. Grant."

When Leroy opened the door, releasing a blade of yellow light, Charlie saw his partner had his eyes open - a good sign. Charlie knelt down beside D.S. Harris.

"You hurt?"

Harris blinked, the light from Leroy's apartment making his eyes smart. The left side of his face felt thick, slightly swollen. Other than that he felt a little groggy, but basically okay, and said as much.

Charlie looked carefully at his partner, checking for cuts and bruises, making sure Tony Harris's eyes stayed focused on him.

"Stay down a minute, get yourself together, then we'll drive over to A & E and get you checked out properly."

"No need. I'm okay." Tony Harris' tongue worked at the dryness inside his mouth. The anxiety he'd felt waiting outside, then riding up to the ninth floor, had gone. "I was waiting like you said, just waiting and watching, when something spooked the man. I came towards him, then, I'd got no other choice, and Blackstock slammed the door. Suddenly it was dark, the man rushed past me, and somehow I went over. This's a hard floor and it stunned me, but I'm not hurt. If that piece of shit Blackstock hadn't slammed the fucking door there'd've been no problem."

Harris stood up. Used his hands to iron out the creases in his suit. He pointed at Leroy.

"That piece of shit bottled!"

Charlie decided not to ask any more questions, nodding his head as if he accepted his partner's account then turning to look at Leroy.

Leroy's face was wet with tears. Restlessly, he moved his head back and forth, back and forth.

"Leroy, are you hurt?" Charlie asked.

"I'm dead is what I am," Leroy said, still moving his head.

Charlie was hot. He palmed sweat from his brow then stood so close to Leroy he smelled the Special Brew on his breath.

"The prick slammed the door!" Harris snapped. When he stepped away from the wall, Harris saw Leroy flinch and knew he wouldn't contradict him in front of Charlie.

"Leroy?" Charlie said, his voice low. "We need to talk. Sort some stuff out." Leroy didn't look like he intended to be hospitable, so Charlie added: "It's not such a good idea to talk out here, and have people listening in."

Leroy dragged the sleeve of the hooded top across his face before looking wildly up and down the corridor.

"Best we come inside," Charlie said. He turned to Tony Harris: "You sure you're okay?"

"I'm fine," Harris said, fixing Leroy with a filthy look as he stepped into the flat.

Following Leroy through the hall into the living room, Charlie knew the muscles in his legs were going to be sore as a result of running up those stairs. He sighed, but the prospect of sore muscles wasn't why. Leroy used H. He'd been nicked so many times – possession; theft; disorderly conduct; causing a public nuisance - his record read like a book of short stories. Setting up this pinch, Charlie'd said nothing when Leroy told him he didn't know much about the guy he bought his H from - not his name, not where he lived: just that the guy'd only been in business six months, maybe a year, was still practically a stranger. It was all twenty-two carat bullshit, but Charlie'd let it go because Leroy was helping out.

The plan was to watch the purchase and bag the dealer. Leroy's co-operation would help out with the case he had pending. With the dealer and Leroy both serving time it wouldn't occur to anybody that Leroy'd grassed.

Neat and sweet is how things should've worked out.

But they hadn't.

"Mr. Grant, you got to see Gregory, that's the truth."

The three men were crowded into the living room: threadbare rugs on white plastic tiles, grey woodchip on the walls, a threadbare settee opposite the window. There were no curtains, so you got a view of the night sky or, if you got closer, the Estate: the funfair without fun. Leroy sat down. Charlie stood with his back to the window. Tony Harris stood in the doorway, looking shaken and angry.

"I say," Leroy said, "I want some H, and Gregory says he knows a guy, and he'll speak to him, send the guy over to see me. On my life, that's all I know."

Charlie looked over at Leroy's CD player, on the floor by the window. Took the time to squat down and flick through Leroy's CDs. He believed you could tell things about a person from the music they listened to, but what Leroy's taste in music said about him Charlie didn't know because he recognised none of the names on the CDs. He stood, slowly, conscious of the lactic acid in his thighs, and watched Leroy reach for the can of Special Brew, then take two long swallows, his Adams' apple and the four-inch long horizontal scar above it, bobbing.

"Leroy," Charlie said, "I look at your music and I don't know anybody. But I'm thirty-six years old so you don't expect me to, right?"

Leroy took another drink. He liked the taste, but…There were two coppers in his flat: one standing in the doorway, looking like he wanted to rip him up, the other eyeballing his CDs then asking him crazy questions. The Special Brew was okay, but he needed a hit, needed to be out of his skull.

"Yeah," Charlie said, answering his own question. "Now, if I'd got the time, and I wasn't so tired, I could stand here all night and let you tell me you don't know your dealer. Let you tell me Gregory - he's the one who knows him. Then go see Gregory and have him tell me you made a mistake - you got him mixed up with Billy. Or Andrea. Or Michelle. I could go on like that. I could visit all the users on the Estate. As if I was on a tour. What I'd find is none of them knows anything. If I'd got the time, if I'd got the energy, maybe it'd be fun, but I don't."

Impatient, Tony Harris looked away. As far as he was concerned, Blackstock was scum, in and out of institutions - a human yo-yo - and the best way to deal with scum was to cut the preamble and say: "This is what I want to know, I'm going to start counting, and if I get to three and you don't give me what I want, I'll bust your fucking jaw you piece of shit!" But Grant, Tony Harris saw, hadn't the ability to see things in black and white, which accounted for him being thirty-six and still a D.S. That was Grant's problem. Harris felt it could be worked to his advantage.

Leroy said, "I see your point, Mr. Grant."

"So, tell me the name of the man who came to sell."

Leroy squirmed. He looked up at the ceiling - where the paint had cracked and started to flake off - then out at the night sky. It was a clear night and he could see the stars. He said:

"Harry."

"Where's Harry live?" Charlie asked.

Leroy screwed up his eyes. He knew the Special Brew was all gone, but he shook the can anyway. When he got nervous, he stuttered and this line of questions made him very nervous: " I d-don't-"

"You're lying," Charlie said. "You've known me what: two, three years?"

Leroy nodded.

"I've been working the Estate three years now and you think I don't know the score?" Leroy lowered his eyes and waited for Charlie to continue. "The dealers make their money off the people on the Estate. You want Crack, Coke, H, Acid,

11

whatever, the dealers've got it, or they'll get it. It's a simple equation - they sell, you buy. The real key is speed: When you start to itch do you send for mail order H? I don't think so. You make a call, you talk to somebody, and a deal's done. For that to happen the dealers've got to be close by and easy to get hold of. You think I've worked this Estate for three years and I'm so stupid I don't know how things operate? Is that what you think, Leroy?"

"I know you're not stupid." Leroy fingered the empty can. D.S. Grant wasn't stupid, but that wasn't the issue here - the issue as far as Leroy was concerned was his balls: Leroy'd heard all about the way Harry operated from Tommy Morrison: Tommy got into some kind of argument with Harry. They were at Tommy's house. They had words and Harry asked if he could use the phone. "Harry," Tommy'd said, "knows phone companies have records, and he knows people can get busted when they make phone calls if the police get hold of the records, so he borrows somebody else's phone when he needs to make a call." Tommy'd shrugged and said sure Harry could use the phone. Harry'd made a call and ten minutes later College had arrived. Harry'd got out a Stanley knife and College had held Tommy. Harry'd used the Stanley knife to slice off Tommy's right ball. "I know what you're thinking," Tommy'd said. "One guy's holding me, the other's got a knife, but even so: why don't I struggle? I tell you, man, when you're in a situation like that, everything's different from the way you imagined it'd be. Bruce Willis isn't there to help out! Harry told me he was going to cut off one of my balls. It wasn't negotiable. He said he'd cut off one ball and as far as he was concerned, we'd be even. Said to show what a nice guy he was, he was going to leave me my left ball unless I struggled, in which case he'd cut off both my balls. I thought about it. Harry looked as if he'd be happy if I struggled. I decided to keep still." Leroy shuddered. The thought of what'd happen if Harry found out he'd grassed, scared him shitless.

"You're worried," Charlie said. "And I understand that. You said earlier you were dead, and it can happen, I know it, you know it."

The longer this went on, the more Leroy needed a hit. Grant was okay for a copper - he didn't shit you around and tried, if he could, to help you out. Yet Grant scared him, too. He wasn't a big guy, didn't shout, didn't have crazy eyes like Harry, or wild eyes like College, but Leroy could see if push came to shove Grant wouldn't back down.

"We should've bagged Harry, like we arranged," Charlie admitted. "It didn't happen, and I'd be a liar if I said you hadn't got some cause to worry about what might be running through Harry's mind now or sometime soon, be a liar if I stood here and told you this stuff wasn't dangerous."

Leroy passed one of his hands over his jaw. He swallowed. Then he glanced over at the copper in the doorway.

"Prick!" Harris mouthed when he saw he had Leroy's attention. He needed to piss. It was hard for him to let Grant keep talking. He decided Grant talked so much because talking was all he was good for.

"If you and Harry were both serving time, you for your case pending, him for dealing, what happened he'd have put down to bad luck: he deals, you buy, you both get tumbled, you both serve time, it's an occupational hazard. But we missed him, Leroy. So sooner or later Harry's going to start wondering how it was that he happened to be selling on the ninth floor of a block of flats, it's nearly midnight, and two coppers just happen to turn up. He'll start wondering and, my guess is: he'll want a chat with you.

"Your best bet, the way I see it, is to tell us where Harry lives. So tomorrow we can follow him till he sells to someone else. Then we can bag him and you can rest easy."

Though he wasn't drunk, Leroy was starting to feel hung over, the pain worse when he tried to sort out his head - get a few things straight.

"What if," Leroy managed after a pause, "tomorrow he d-doesn't d-do any d-deals? Where's that leave me?"

"If we follow him tomorrow and we don't see him make any deals, two things'll happen. One: I'll come back and take you out of here – get you somewhere else to stay till things are sorted. And two: things will be sorted. If Harry doesn't do any deals tomorrow, we'll get a warrant and dig out Harry's stash. We'll arrest him for dealing, but without actually seeing it done, and with no previous, Harry'll get off with possession. If that happens Harry'll get a suspended sentence only, which he won't connect with you."

"If I t-tell you Harry's address you'll go?" Kenny T. lived in MacMillan House, behind Churchill House. Kenny T. cut his stuff so much people only went to him as a last resort, but that *was* the case: Leroy's head was hurting, his nose was starting to run. Pretty soon he'd get the shakes. He needed to get there quickly because if Kenny T. saw him shaking, Kenny 'd up the price.

"You tell me his address and we're out of here," Charlie agreed.

"Harry lives on Segemore Street, on the edge of the Estate, just up the road from The G-Green Man."

"Number?"

Leroy frowned. He was starting to come apart, his fingers squeezing the empty can. "Seven! Number seven!"

13

Arms held slightly away from his sides, D.S. Tony Harris led them out of Churchill House and over to his car, a blue Mondeo. After ten minutes of silence, his eyes on the road ahead, Harris said:

"Allison'll be awake when I get in." He let that sink in before he added: "You're divorced, right?"

"Yeah."

"What happened must've pissed you off."

The first time Charlie met his new partner, as they were shaking hands – and it was nothing he'd heard, nothing to do with the way Harris looked or sounded, just instinct - it came to him that Tony Harris was a shit. "It's fair to say I wasn't chuffed," Charlie admitted.

The second week with Charlie, when Tony Harris found out his new partner's brother was the C.I. in Benbury, and that there was a promotion up for grabs, Harris'd made it his business to find out as much about his new partner as he could.

"I heard he moved down south. I heard he's a C.I. now."

Charlie'd heard so, too. You heard those things whether you wanted to or not. He looked out the window. He was tired, and the streetlights hurt his eyes, but he kept looking at them anyway.

"Do you ever hear from her?"

"No," Charlie said. "If you don't have kids..." Charlie gripped his knees. He didn't seem to be explaining this very well. Not that it mattered: he was pretty sure Tony Harris wasn't asking out of any real interest, and certainly not out of concern. "We didn't have any kids," he said, and left it at that. They didn't have any kids, though for over a year they'd tried. Then they'd found he wasn't able to, found his balls had been broken as well as his left wrist: Charlie knew then it was a mistake to think you could outdistance your past: it came back to haunt you. Haunted was how he felt right now. All at once he was close to tears. The streetlights became fuzzy. Thinking about Louise, about the final year they spent together, hurt him, that why he tried hard not to think about her.

"It's started snowing," Tony Harris said. He seemed happy, now.

Still caught up by his memories, Charlie watched the snowflakes gathering on the glass. He and Louise had wanted kids. But it hadn't happened, couldn't ever happen. "You and your wife need to discuss the alternatives," the doctor who'd confirmed his infertility had said. The doctor was young. Gave the impression he knew everything, though when he'd smiled and said, "This isn't the end of the road," he'd been wrong: it was the end for Charlie and Louise, though it'd taken them a whole year to come right out and say it, a year of him sleeping downstairs

14

on the settee, wishing he had X-ray vision so he could see through the ceiling, see if Louise was awake too, believing if she was there was still hope for them, but if she was asleep, they were finished. That long year, all those nights awake on the settee, all the bitter words they exchanged whenever their energy levels nudged up off ground zero, Charlie could have done without. Just thinking about it made his balls ache. Louise had started seeing Hutchinson. "It's love," she said when she got around to telling him. By then it wasn't news: the whole station knew. She'd divorced him and married Hutchinson; they'd moved, and Hutchinson had been promoted. Charlie accepted all this – he had no choice - but he wasn't over it. Blinking, he said:

"I'm hungry, I need to get something from the All-Night shop. If you drop me off by the Hawthorns School, that'll be great."

"I'll pick you up in the morning," Tony Harris said, stopping right outside the school, the Victorian building dusted with white.

A semi, with a red-tiled roof, three bedrooms, gardens front and back, and a garage, the house had been built in the mid-fifties and was solid, though - lightly coated with snow - it looked as ethereal as the Hawthorns School. Charlie let himself in and marked his passage through to the kitchen with electric light. In the All-Night shop he'd been so sure of his hunger he'd scooped three microwave meals from the deep freeze. But during the short walk home his appetite had deserted him. Now he settled for tea, drinking it standing in the kitchen, staring out the window at the back garden, at the snow closing in on him, all the time thinking about Louise: Last Christmas he'd bought her a card, though he hadn't sent it. It was buried amongst the various papers strewn across the kitchen table. Maybe he'd sort it out and send it this Christmas, just a few days away, though he didn't think he'd be able to... In the first place, he didn't have her address. And in the second place, the steaming Christmas pudding on the front of the card reminded him of -

"Stop it!"

Louise was with Hutchinson, married - embroiled in a new life. These were the facts. Just put it away, Charlie told himself, knowing he couldn't, knowing though he was good and tired it'd be a mistake to go to bed with his head this full.

So, after drinking his tea he put on a grey sweat suit and a pair of Reeboks and went through the kitchen to the garage. He reversed the Fiesta out onto the drive. Snow fell soundlessly through halos of sodium light. Wasn't orange meant to be a warm colour? Charlie thought it was, yet the orange-painted snow sent a chill through him and he hurried back inside, pulling the steel door down after him.

The fluorescent threw harsh light over the newspapers stacked at the side of the garage, the shelves of rusting tools at its rear, the black leather punch bag hanging from the exposed central beam. From a brass hook on the back of the door to the kitchen he took: a skipping rope, leather mitts, and a stopwatch. With the car outside, the smell of leather cut through the mingled stink of petrol and engine oil.

Reeboks slapping lightly against the concrete floor, Charlie skipped for three minutes, then took thirty seconds rest, pacing up and down with the rope draped around his neck, his head bent forwards. Skip then rest, skip then rest: three minutes of effort followed by thirty seconds of rest, his efforts timed, exact, ritualistic.

After six rounds of skipping he hung up the rope, put on the mitts, and hit the punch bag for three minutes, throwing single punches till his shoulders loosened, then flurries of jabs, hooks, uppercuts, concentrating his effort, timing the back-swing of the bag, keeping his hands high the way he'd been taught. During the rest period, he strode up and down with his hands on his hips while the bag pendulumed, the iron chain from which it was suspended, creaking. Focused wholly on what he was doing, Charlie drove himself to hit the bag harder and faster, the sound of each impact exploding in his ears. Sweat dripped from the end of his nose. The fire in his lungs spread to his chest. Hit and move, hit and move. Exhilarated by his own efforts, he began dipping from the hips to get his full weight behind each shot, pushing it until his left wrist spoke up, its voice sharp and clear. Charlie removed the mitts then and massaged his left wrist with his right hand, squeezing hard, as if to throttle the pain. He'd been stupid to hit with such abandon not least because the pain in his wrist drove him deeper into the past, though that was later, in a dream that tangled the duvet but didn't survive till dawn.

# FOUR

Her neck and shoulders prickly with heat despite the cold, Rachel Grant backed her car out of the garage. The Peugeot 106 held the road well and the way the snow was coming down it'd have to. When Dennis'd told her he didn't need her, "not tonight, not ever" she hadn't been surprised and now, driving aimlessly - through a residential area, past a shopping complex - Rachel considered this.

In Dennis there was no give. He was the star player, his career the play. She was just a prop. These things were clear, undeniable…which forced the question: What kind of future was it for her?

It wasn't any kind of future! And the truth was she'd known it for some time, that why she hadn't been surprised by what Dennis'd said. Rachel had kidded herself that things could be worked out, making believe it was just a matter of time until things came right, until they lived happily ever after. That she'd clung so tenaciously to such notions made her angry. She should have cut and run a long time ago.

Traffic was light. A city-dweller, at any other time Rachel would have drawn pleasure from that fact, but tonight she was adrift from her usual concerns. Moving into the fast lane, she accelerated to 80mph, and imagined herself suddenly losing control, the car flipping over, steel twisting its way through her flesh, the warm rush of pain.

That she didn't care, at this moment, if she lived or died, was, Rachel knew, a guarantee she wouldn't die tonight. Call it Sod's law. Doing 80, on a snow-covered motorway, at night, tired and angry, she was safe. But if, healed and hopeful, she was driving carefully along some side road, late afternoon sunlight slanting through the windscreen - a truck might rage into her without warning, bringing instant death.

Wasn't that a cheerful thought?

Oddly, it seemed to be, and Rachel smiled. With her free hand she switched on the radio. More snow was on its way. After the forecast, Cher sang *Gypsies, Tramps and Thieves*. Rachel wondered what Cher'd do if she were in her shoes, decided she'd stop for coffee.

At a little after 2AM Rachel pulled onto the motorway services. Though the car was already three-quarters full, she put in more petrol. The attendant, a grizzled little man with nicotine stained fingers, looked her up and down, grinned and said:

"Nice night!"

Rachel frowned, then realised she had on only the sleeveless black dress she'd worn at the Convention Centre. Cher'd have probably countered with a wisecrack, but Rachel's mind stayed resolutely blank, leaving her to push her change into her purse and hurry back to her car, parking as near the entrance to the cafeteria as possible.

A few professional insomniacs, and travellers, all worn looking, sat drinking coffee and reading the early editions of morning newspapers - stealing a head start on the rest of the world. None of them stirred when Rachel entered, and the waitress managed to serve her without actually looking at her at all, for which she was grateful. Wrapping her hands around the polystyrene cup for warmth, Rachel sat at a table by the window, as far from everyone else as possible, intent on avoiding stray conversation.

Made fuzzy by the falling snow, the motorway seemed mysterious, full of possibility, as it had when she was a child. Rachel remembered being nine years old and looking out of a window much like this one, watching the other cars, wondering where they'd been and where they were heading. Now she could play the game with herself: Where have I been? Where am I heading?

Before Rachel could press for an answer, a woman's voice broke in on her thoughts:

"The coffee here's terrible," it announced.

When she'd scanned the cafeteria before sitting, Rachel had noticed the other customers were all men. Strange - but she told herself it didn't matter.

"The coffee's terrible, but these places are good for getting your mind going. Just now I was thinking about my dad. He had an affair with his secretary. Joan was her name. She was twenty-five. She wore thigh length plastic boots and bright coloured tops. She had a cast in her left eye. I always felt she was watching me."

Rachel pushed her cup sharply away, and still the voice barely drew breath before it continued:

"I was fourteen when mom and dad divorced. I remember mom leaving more clearly than I remember what happened yesterday. She packed everything into a dust-covered suitcase and stood it in the hallway. I wanted it to be raining, cold, miserable, but sunlight shone through the stained glass fan above the front door, and a bird sang outside. For a second or two they stood looking at each other. Neither of them spoke. Then mom bent down, picked up her suitcase, and lugged it out to the taxi.

"It was best for me to stay with my dad, mom'd said. Really, though, I knew she left me there as a way of getting back at him.

18

"A month after the divorce, I slept with Billy Payne and, knowing he couldn't stand to hear it, I told dad all about it. He packed my clothes into two holdalls, and said I was going to stay with my mom. He said: it'd all been arranged.

"I met Joan again just over a year ago. Her hair was short and she was wearing baggy clothes to hide that she'd put on weight. Her face was lined and puffy. We stood outside WH Smiths, crowds of Saturday shoppers bustling by. "What I did," she said, "I did because I loved your dad. You were the slut, doing what you did just to hurt him. I hope you suffer!" she said. I've never heard anyone say the word "suffer" the way she said it."

Rachel scanned the cafeteria. She saw everyone was staring. She stood up. Her tongue felt thick and bitter tasting. She placed her hands on the table for support.

The waitress came over from the service counter. She looked like a nurse.

"Are you alright?"

Only hours before, in another life, she'd been asked the same question by another waitress. Now it seemed even more important to lie:

"I'm fine," she said, deciding to escape when the waitress spoke to the woman who'd joined her.

But there was no woman.

"Where'd she go?"

The waitress blanked her.

"The woman who sat talking to me," Rachel explained, her words frantic, garbled.

Back in her car Rachel echoed the waitresses' response:

"You were talking to yourself."

The snow was still falling. Resisting the desire to chew her fingers, Rachel drove back to Benbury.

"Did you really curse me, Joan?" she wondered aloud, indicating when she saw the sign for Junction 2.

19

FIVE

Harry smoked like a man who's watched too many movies, each gesture exaggerated for dramatic effect. Sprawled on the chair opposite the TV, a video playing, he killed the sound so he could catch College's joke:

"This guy, right, he's got this woman on his bed and he puts a carrot up her cunt, right, and she goes: Ahhh, ahhh! Then he gets a banana, right, and he puts that up her cunt, and she goes: Ahhh, ahhh! Then he gets one of those...you know...those long green vegetables...what're they called?"

"Cucumbers," Manraj volunteered.

"You've played the game before!" College said, breaking into giggles.

Harry smiled. Then directed his attention back at the TV, turning the volume so high he had to shout to be heard:

"This's fucking brilliant!"

Drawing deeply on his cigarette, he watched intently as Bruce Lee used two clubs to kill or maim half a dozen men, scowling and screaming each time he struck a blow. When the sequence ended – with Lee imprisoned by steel doors in an underground cavern, Harry killed the sound again.

"You see that?"

Manraj nodded.

"Fast, man!" Harry let out a short, appreciative whistle.

"Yeah," College agreed, balling his hands into fists.

Seeing this, Harry sat up and cracked his knuckles.

"Come on, then."

"No way!"

Harry laughed, relishing the compliment.

"This's my best video. The best Bruce Lee film. I've seen it at least a hundred times. *Fist Of Fury*'s next best. Then *Big Boss*, then *Way Of The Dragon*."

"You seen *Game Of Death*?"

"Watched it ten times with you, twat! Seen it about thirty times altogether. It's crap."

Kerry came in. Bone-thin, her long, fine brown hair in disarray, she looked lost and confused. With the fire on full, it was hot in the low-ceilinged room, yet Kerry wrapped her arms around herself and shivered. Her leather jacket, the same as those worn by Harry, College and Manraj, accentuated the waxy paleness of her skin. Eyes unfocussed, she stared at the blue-orange flames, waiting.

"You know where it is," Harry snapped. He'd watched *Enter The Dragon* twice back to back and still he didn't feel right. He hadn't felt right since his run

20

in with the copper in Churchill House. "Roll four," he said. He told everyone: when he clicked his fingers, Kerry opened her legs - the way it should be - but rolling joints was where her real talent lay, and right now a joint was just what he needed to help him chill.

Kerry looked at him but didn't move.

"Today!" Harry yelled. When she left the room he added: "Thick bitch!"

College grinned on cue. Manraj kept his face impassive.

"You think she's only here for the gear, right?"

"I don't think nothing."

"Yeah you do." Harry grinned. "But I don't give a shit what nobody thinks." He shrugged to emphasize his indifference. Drummed his fingers on the arm of the chair, watching Manraj closely. Harry found it difficult to read Manraj. Whereas with College you knew where you were.

They watched the movie until Kerry came in and handed out expertly rolled joints. Harry moved his gold lighter before each face in turn, the tear of flame briefly illuminating: Kerry's washed out eyes, Manraj's scarred lips, College's pockmarked cheeks. Then Harry added commentary:

"Watch the kicks...Now he breaks the guy's neck...Look at the combinations...Look at the stomach muscles." When the sequence ended, he stood and unzipped his jacket, raised his black tee shirt to reveal his own stomach. "You think I'm getting fat?" He looked at Kerry.

"No," she answered. She smiled. Not yet twenty, Kerry'd been raped by her father when she was twelve, then spent three years in care; she chain smoked and her face was lined from squinting, but when she smiled, she was a child again.

"Liar," Harry said, tugging at his flesh to make a point. "I think I'm going to start working out again. Maybe we'll go to the gym sometime this week. Just because a man sells gear, don't mean he's got to be unhealthy, does it?" He nodded, suggesting something had been settled. Then he sat down and patted his thigh.

Obediently, Kerry sat on his lap, moving to kiss him, knowing he needed to show off, though not what had ignited the need.

His eyes open, Harry let her press her lips against his. When she'd finished, he sent her into the kitchen to make coffee, snapping at her for the fun of it.

College smiled to show his appreciation of the control. Manraj didn't.

"If I didn't like you," Harry told Manraj, "I wouldn't let you look at me that way. I don't like being looked at or touched." Locating a spot just below his hairline, he squeezed it till it burst. "If my wife's family found me here with

Kerry..." He grinned. "My wife's brother killed a guy. Gutted him with a butcher knife. If they found me here, it's what they'd do to me...Leastways they'd try."

Manraj nodded, but Harry wasn't sure Manraj knew how good he was, which could be a problem. In his business, fear was the key. Fear kept everyone in line. Without fear, he was lost.

Finished with his joint, Harry let his eyes slip out of focus. But he wasn't chilled. Again he went over what'd happened inside Churchill House: The first copper'd gone down like a sack of shit, a big guy but fat, and so scared it was funny. But the second copper...Normally, when you went for them, people folded like a piece of paper, the fat copper being a case in point. Or else they got scared and they rushed you, shouting, screaming, wild. But the second copper was different. It'd been dark. The second copper hadn't been able to see him - knew he was there but couldn't see him and still he stood his ground: somebody who didn't back down. Harry'd been doing business on the Estate for over a year. He knew when the coppers needed to bust somebody they busted users, who were easy to find, and didn't put up a fight. The arrangement made the coppers look good and it suited Harry. Only it wasn't how the cool copper saw things.

When the credits rolled, Harry snapped off the TV and stood up.

"I told you I had a run in with two coppers. They're going to be coming here."

"How d'you know?" College asked.

Harry pushed his hands into his pockets. The knowledge was part of the reason he'd felt shitty. He didn't know how he knew they'd find their way here – he just knew. What'd happened inside Churchill House was the start of something - Harry saw that now.

"I just know," Harry said, and bent to eject the video, sliding it into its case, ready to take. He looked at Manraj, still watching him, his face not giving anything away.

"We got to run?" Manraj asked.

Harry grinned.

"The way you talk, it's a good thing I like you." With his fingertips Harry explored the site of the spot he'd exploded. "Kerry," he called, turning away from Manraj. When she put her head around the door he saw she'd rolled herself a fresh joint. He made a mental note to communicate with Kerry once they'd left the house - nothing too heavy: he'd just smack her once then ask: "Who the fuck do you think you are?" "Forget the coffee," he said. "Put the gear into the green sports bags."

"All of it?"

"Yeah."

22

Harry turned to look at Manraj again, sitting low on his spine, his legs stretched out before him.

"Are we going somewhere?" Kerry asked, still by the door, taking a pull of her joint then flicking strands of hair off her face.

Staring down at Manraj, Harry said:

"We'll stay at Manny's house for a few days." Still Manraj's face didn't give anything away. Now the TV was off, it was almost completely dark, the way it'd been when the cool copper came at him. Fear was the key. Harry looked at Manraj. He looked at College. Users, other dealers, cops, even your own guys…if you wanted them to stay in line they had to be scared of you. "Just till I sort things."

"You going to sort out coppers?" Manraj asked.

Harry saw he had College's attention, too. He grinned, his teeth visible even in the near darkness.

"It'd be a mistake to do nothing."

Twenty minutes later they were getting into the year old BMW parked on the street in front of the house, the gear in green sports bags. In the movie *Heat* Robert DeNiro played a gangster who said you had to be able to walk away from everything and everyone. Harry liked that, and the fact that he'd been able to pack and go in just twenty minutes, made him feel good, the best he'd felt since leaving Churchill House.

After locking the front door, Harry spoke to College:

"Reach into the dash, see if there's a Stanley in there."

College did as he was told.

"A new one," College said. He fished it out and handed it to Harry, who slid out the blade.

He knelt, and placed the Stanley knife on the step. It was still snowing, but the step was enclosed - Harry didn't think it'd get covered over.

"What's that about?" College asked.

Harry got in.

"You've heard of Email, right?"

"Yeah."

"Well I just left some Stanley-mail!"

# SIX

December 19th

When Dennis Grant woke - almost 7.05AM – Rachel wasn't there. He put on his dressing gown and checked downstairs, expecting to find her asleep on the settee or making coffee in the kitchen, her face a mile long - as if she was the one who had a right to be pissed off, conveniently managing to forget how she'd tried to destroy his speech.

But Rachel wasn't in the house, and when Dennis checked the garage he saw her car was gone. When she was pissed off, she drove; it was something she'd done before and would do again when Dennis got around to telling her he'd had a vasectomy. She'd come back sooner or later. Her parents were dead, she'd never mentioned any other family, and if Rachel had friends she'd managed to keep them a secret. The long and short of it was: Dennis knew Rachel had only him. She worked, but the money she earned wouldn't go far. When they were first married, Dennis'd told her to chuck her job, believing it'd be for the best if she concentrated on entertaining the brass. But she wouldn't have it, insisted she needed some independence. Dennis had pointed out her job didn't pay enough for her to be independent, but she'd made her mind up. If Rachel tried to stay away very long, she'd see he was right about that. The thought was a comfort to him.

Dennis drank a cup of strong, very sweet coffee and ate two slices of toast spread thickly with margarine. It was starting to get light. He glanced out the front window. Keen Close looked like a Christmas card. He saw the FOR SALE in the middle of the lawn of number 12 and made a mental note to phone the estate agent to ask the price – this a way of gauging the value of his own property. If he got £150,000 for this place, after his promotion he'd be able to buy something really top drawer.

When he'd dried himself from his shower, Dennis took one of the transparent plastic tubes from his dresser, warmed it with his hands and carried it into the bathroom. Careful to hurt himself - still unable to achieve full hardness - Dennis masturbated, ejaculating into the tube. The white-tiled bathroom made his semen look grey. He was sure it hadn't always been that colour. Capping the tube, Dennis placed it on top of the cabinet whilst he shaved. His come had changed colour. None of the leaflets he'd read about the operation had said anything about that. He wondered if the taste had changed, too. It'd be something if, before he dropped the sample off at the hospital, he bumped into Kay Bevington: "Hello,

24

Kay, long time no see. Listen, I've just had a vasectomy and I'd like you to help me out: Taste this...Tell me if the taste's changed." The bitch had said she was sucking him just to get him ready, but she'd made him come so he'd look a fool. Dennis'd been seventeen. Kay'd been twenty. He'd called her a slut, but that wasn't why she'd started crying - she'd cried, Dennis knew, because he'd seen through her, seen she was out to belittle him, telling her friends how quickly he'd come, then laughing, Kay and her friends, all of them laughing at him. Mascara'd run down her face. He'd been tempted to give the little slut something to *really* remember him by. But even then Dennis had been smart enough to know that if he hit her and it got out, it'd hurt him later.

Dennis put on aftershave - Old Spice, the same as the old man'd used. With a towel wrapped around his waist, he went into the bedroom. He put on a white button down shirt, a grey silk tie, and a dark blue suit. Then he drove to the hospital.

## SEVEN

"I'm sorry."

"Don't be. Come in." Charlie, in grey tee shirt and sweatpants, led her through to the living room.

"I woke you."

"I'm glad you did." He pushed his fingers through his hair, giving himself time to think. He could see something was wrong. "Coffee?"

"I should go."

"It's instant - but it's not that bad!"

Rachel didn't smile. Seemed confused. Charlie said:

"Bad joke. Never mind. Come on."

Slowly, as if she were sleepwalking, she followed him into the kitchen. He pushed away papers to clear a space at the table, then made them both coffee, sipping his own when it was still very hot.

Her eyes on the steam rising from her mug, Rachel said:

"I've left him."

Charlie sat down. He'd slept maybe two hours. To show he'd heard, that he'd understood, he nodded.

"Dennis is your brother, I shouldn't be here - I don't know what I was thinking."

He tore kitchen towel from the roll. Rachel thought they were to wipe up the coffee she'd spilled, a lake of it, expanding towards the pile of papers he'd cleared. Instead he handed her the towel. Only then did she realise she was crying.

"This is all junk," he said, feeding the dripping papers - and the Christmas card he'd never sent - into the bin before mopping up the spilled coffee. "I've been meaning to throw it away."

She looked at him, his hands wet with coffee.

"It's okay," he said. "Really."

The kitchen was smaller than the one back at the house - she thought of it as 'the house', not as a home, much less her home - but she felt comfortable in it.

"I need to make a phone call – so I won't have to run off right away, then I'll go for take two with the coffee!" He added: "When I say stuff like that: at least give me a smile."

Done wiping away her tears, Rachel obliged.

"Two minutes," Charlie said, and went to make his call.

# EIGHT

Tony Harris hung up.

"D.I. Grant," he explained. "He says I needn't pick him up. Says he'll use his own car - come in later."

Allison Harris finished working her dark hair into a French plait before dipping a chocolate biscuit into her tea, her eyes on her husband.

"Don't wait for him," she said. "This's your chance." Her tongue speared a fleck of chocolate from her fingertip.

Tony Harris worked his shirt into his trousers, adjusted his jacket. When he got the promotion, he was going to get a new suit - one with plenty of room in it.

"Maybe you're right," Harris said. He crossed the kitchen to help out with the chocolate biscuits, chewing fast, swallowing hard.

Last night when he'd got home Allison hadn't been watching the Sherlock Holmes movie as he'd anticipated - she'd been making pancakes. They'd eaten them with raspberry jam and cream and Harris had told her - most of - what had happened at Churchill House.

"All I know about him's what you've told me," Allison said. "He's thirty-six. His younger brother is the C.I. He's got a reputation as a good copper, but something must be wrong with him or else he'd've been promoted already. You do things right, make a good impression and this promotion'll be yours. Remember the golden rule: Sell yourself: It's not what you do, it's what you say you do."

The biscuits were all gone.

"I don't give free consultations, by the way," Allison Harris added.

"Bill me!"

"Rest assured," she said.

Charlie Grant'd said on the phone that Tony Harris should watch Leroy's place - to make sure Harry didn't pay a return call, curious about why some coppers had turned up at Leroy's flat at midnight. Did Charlie think he couldn't go after Harry alone? Harris wondered. Or was Charlie playing the game a little himself – his eye on the promotion, too?

"I prefer the Hobnobs," Harris said. He pointed at the crumpled wrapper, and made a mental note to get a couple of packets.

NINE

Charlie Grant parked in the compound at the rear of the Benbury Police Station - high brick walls fringed with barbed wire. Cold winds knifing through his black wool suit, he hurried inside, telling himself to stay focused on what he had to do - get the phone number of Leroy's brother from his desk; then go to Churchill House - speak with Tony, see what was happening.

But staying focused wasn't easy. Rachel had told him she wasn't ever going back - things were over between her and Dennis. He'd left Rachel a key - it'd been Louise's key, but Charlie told himself he mustn't think of it that way anymore: Louise was gone, it was *just a key*. He'd told Rachel she could stay as long as she wanted - the bed in the spare room was already made up. "Thanks," she'd said. When she'd taken the key off him she'd said: "You like me?" What she needed, Charlie decided, was a confidence boost. Hence her question, and his reply: "I like you." Only now Charlie wasn't so sure it had been a question. In replay it was an observation: "You like me."

"C.I. wants to see you," Frank Connor said. Frank, the desk sergeant, was a thickset man with dark hair shot through with grey.

Charlie grimaced. The other thing he meant to do while he was at the station was see Dennis, tell him he'd heard from Rachel - leaving it vague, like that - he'd 'heard from her'...not: she was staying at his house.

But Charlie wanted to see Dennis of his own accord - he didn't want to be summoned.

Victorian, the station had been modernised to accommodate late twentieth century technology, the modernisation highlighting the gloom of oak-panelled walls, iron stair rails, and the expression on Charlie's face.

He took his time, each step defining the residue of the previous day's exertions, deciding if Dennis got heavy about it he'd say: "Rachel's my sister-in-law - she came to my door, she needed help, should I have turned her away?" Was that the right way to say it? Was it?

Charlie knocked. Waited...

"Come in," Dennis called.

Unready, Charlie stepped inside.

Redecorated more than a year ago, the C.I.'s office still smelled of new paint. Dennis Grant stared out at the pound and Benbury beyond it, the town centre snow-covered, a mix of Victorian buildings and Sixties haute couture.

Charlie was still trying to figure out how to say what he wanted to say when Dennis spoke, turning to look at him only at the end of his first sentence:

"I need you to help me out here. It won't be easy for you, but I want you to do your best."

Charlie knew then it'd be a mistake to mention Rachel.

"I've been looking through the figures." Dennis pointed at the computer on his desk, light from the screen reflected onto the front of his suit. "You're working the Beeches Farm Estate. It's a cesspool. So, I look to see how many pulls you've made. Hoping to be pleasantly surprised, you supposedly being an experienced D.S."

Dennis turned away again, making Charlie feel like he was back at school - pulled before the class to be ridiculed by the teacher.

"The surprise wasn't pleasant. I'm not happy," he continued, "You're not making enough arrests. End of story."

It was easy to catch little fish, but big fish took longer, was the simple explanation, but Charlie knew to keep his mouth shut.

"What I've just said is on the record," C.I. Dennis Grant said, turning back to the window, the meeting concluded.

Closing the door, Charlie paused to gather himself. Too much was happening at once - Rachel at his house, (*You like me*) Tony Harris looking to wound him with talk of Louise, Harry, the dealer, and now Dennis. What next? Charlie wondered, his head starting to pound.

TEN

After Charlie's phone call Tony Harris drove to the address Leroy had given them: 7 Segemore Street. He parked right out front and looked over at the house, a two-bedroom semi in a state of disrepair – practically identical to the other houses on the Estate. Harris licked his lips, sure if he bagged Harry all by his lonesome, the promotion was his.

It was still early. The curtains to number 7 were drawn. That was good - Harry'd be half awake, easy. Harris popped two Tunes into his mouth - blackcurrant flavour today. He wiped the palms of his hands against his trousers. Some of the fear he'd felt on the ninth floor of Churchill House was back, but he worked it away, telling himself things were different now. It was light for a start, and since Charlie wasn't around, he could get Bobby to lend a hand.

Harris took Bobby from the dashboard. Bobby, named after the man who'd made it, was a present from Allison's father. Half the length of his forearm, lead sandwiched by hard oak, the first time he held Bobby Harris had asked: "What is it?" Allison's father had smiled, winked, and told him it was: "A duck egg tapper!" They'd both laughed at that.

Today was different! It was light and Harry wasn't going to push him aside, not now he had Bobby with him. He'd knock on the door. When Harry opened it, he'd introduce him to Bobby right away. Later, he'd say Harry'd swung at him and he'd reacted.

Harris got out of the car. The snow was thick on the ground. There was a milkman at the top of the street. Harris paused near Harry's door to listen to the rattle of the milk bottles, sharp as the morning air. He gripped Bobby tightly. Using his left hand, he knocked the door. Then he waited, ready as he was ever going to be.

## ELEVEN

What surprised her most was how detached she felt - like she was packing the clothes of some other Rachel Grant - being careful about it, putting things neatly into the suitcase she'd stopped off to buy, believing it was important to start fresh. A couple of times she broke off to look around. The house was cold. Maybe it always had been and she hadn't noticed it till now.

Trying to recall her life with Dennis was like trying to recall details of a nightmare she'd had months, years before. Her stomach tingled with a mixture of anticipation and fear, the tingling intensifying as she hoisted the suitcase into the back of her car.

She was comfortable in blue jeans and blue woollen pullover - having left the black dress she'd worn for Dennis' speech at the Convention Centre spreadeagled on the bed, convinced this was symbolic of something, though what she wasn't sure. She'd taken her clothes, two photograph albums, her building society passbook, assorted other documents. It occurred to her this was the last time she'd ever reverse off this driveway.

It was almost lunchtime and Rachel was hungry. If she stopped to eat in town she might see someone from work. She'd phoned in sick - didn't want to have to say more than that. It was nice and warm in the car. Suddenly she was tempted to keep driving. Why not abandon her old life entirely? Rachel wondered, and thought of Charlie. He liked her. He'd said so. She liked him, too. What was she getting into here? Rachel shuddered. Slowed down so she could work off her wedding ring and slip it into the ashtray - more symbolism, getting a taste for it. What was she getting into? She didn't know. But she was sure she wasn't going to run, for – as if it were preordained - she found herself heading back to Charlie's house.

# TWELVE

"I got here before nine. I sat watching the front door. I'm on my own, what else am I meant to do, right?"

Tony Harris knew Charlie had no answer. That he'd begged off enabled Harris to put Charlie on the spot even though he was lying. The truth was: having found Harry wasn't home Harris had driven over to Churchill House, arriving only ten minutes before Charlie showed up. Then Harris had gone up to Leroy's apartment, figuring Leroy would be able to tell him where else to look for Harry, ready to be persuasive about it – not all talk like his partner...

But Leroy hadn't been home.

"I waited," Harris continued - turning briefly away from Charlie to watch the caretaker drag a refuse bin from the service entrance, chicken bones spilling onto the piss-yellow snow of the forecourt. "But nothing happened. Eventually I decided I better go up there. I knocked on Blackstock's door. There was nobody home." Harris shrugged. "For all we know, he went out after we left and hasn't been back. Or...has this place got a back door?"

"Yeah," Charlie said, wishing his partner's car wasn't so hot – the heater on full, the heat making his eyes feel gritty.

"Maybe Blackstock looked out the window, saw me, and went out the back door."

Another shrug.

It was possible, Charlie acknowledged. If, needing to score, Leroy had seen Tony Harris's car, he'd've gone out the back, down the grass bank surrounding what was left of the playground, past the row of boarded up shops and onto the Estate - like a maze even after you'd worked it for three years. Charlie shook his head. The way Dennis wanted to do things - pulling anybody they could - was a damn sight easier than this. To do this job properly he needed two teams: one to stay and watch Leroy's place, making sure Harry didn't come looking for him; the other to go after Harry. If he asked for backup, Dennis would say no. So...they could stay here and wait for Leroy to come back. Or they could go check out Harry's house. Charlie watched his partner feed two more Tunes into his boiler.

"Let's go check out Harry's place," he said. "He had a late night, he's probably still in bed."

"You're the boss," Harris said.

Harris' smile made Charlie uneasy - a cat that's got the cream smile. If there'd been time, he'd have asked: "Do you know something I don't?"

Charlie parked on The Green Man. And got out of his car.

Harris shut off his engine and rolled down the window. He said:

"I'm happy to stay where I am."

And he wasn't just saying it: he looked happy, seemed to be enjoying himself. Again Charlie wanted to ask: "Do you know something I don't?" But he let it go - flexed his fingers, sucked in cold air

Most of the fences fronting the houses on Segemore Street were broken, allowing snow to gust across front yards and over rusty cars raised on crumbling bricks bleeding oil onto long dead lawns. Harry made enough money to afford better - he chose to live on the Estate, near the action.

When Charlie glanced over at number 7, he knew something was wrong. Downstairs, the curtains were drawn. Upstairs they were open. He walked around to the back of the house. There it was the same story - downstairs the curtains drawn, upstairs: open. He watched for signs of life. Seeing nothing, he picked his way through the back garden and knocked the door. If Harry opened it Charlie'd arrest him for assaulting a police officer and press for a warrant to search the house.

A minute passed before he walked around the side of the house to knock on the front door.

Again: nothing, and Charlie was about to leave when he saw it - partly covered by snow, at the corner of the step. He used his handkerchief to pick up the Stanley knife, brand new, placed on the step so he'd find it...

"You think he left in a hurry?" It didn't mean anything, he was sure, but Harris believed he should have found the knife, was pissed that he hadn't.

Charlie nodded.

"Yeah. But I think he left the knife on purpose. I think Harry knew we'd come looking for him and he wanted to leave a message so we'd know as far as he's concerned, we have unfinished business."

Harris licked his lips and wrestled with that one.

A man paused to let his dog shit on the pavement directly outside Harry's house.

They could stay and watch the house, but Charlie was pretty sure Harry wouldn't return. Back in Churchill House, Tony Harris down, just him and Harry a few feet apart in the dark, Harry hadn't immediately run. That'd been bothering him. It was as if Harry'd been waiting for something. What Harry'd been waiting for, Charlie believed, was his fear, and that he hadn't given him what he wanted, was troubling Harry. That was why he'd left the knife.

" 'Unfinished business' is good," Harris said.

Man and dog stepped away from the steaming conical tower outside Harry's house as Charlie turned to face his partner.

"Good?"

"He'll come to us," Harris explained.

That Tony Harris wasn't concerned about the prospect of Harry coming after them he found disturbing.

"It'd be better," Charlie said, "if we found him."

# THIRTEEN

By mid-afternoon, Dennis Grant was tired. He believed he had a right to be: anybody who thought making a speech was easy had never made one. After ensuring his paperwork was in order, targets for the day, the week, the month all specified, he locked his office and left, telling the desk sergeant to ring him at home if anything important broke, stressing - because Frank Connor was someone who needed things spelled out for him, as dumb as older brother Charlie - that if he was in doubt as to whether a thing was important or not, to ring anyway.

An easy evening was what Dennis had planned: A big meal - food his reward for the work he'd put into his speech - read through a few reports, take another shower, get an early night - taking a sleeping pill if necessary.

Yet as soon as he entered the bedroom, Dennis saw her dresser was empty and knew Rachel had gone. His rage came in waves. He closed his eyes and let it wash over him. Before she'd married him, there'd been others. With him, between Kay Bevington and Rachel there'd been only one other: A bleached blonde with forearms thicker than his own, a cadet he'd met on a survival course when he was still in uniform. She hadn't laughed at him afterwards like Kay, but when she'd called him "Lover boy," he'd caught her tone. Still drunk, the ceiling of her room spiralling, Dennis had waited till she was asleep, lying on her back with her mouth open and snoring like a pig, before dressing and leaving. He hadn't seen her again. Rachel was the first woman Dennis had slept with more than once. That and the fact that he saw her as an aid to his career, had, he was sure, clouded his judgment. Clear to him, now, was that marrying her'd been a mistake. As had letting her give him lip - telling him what she wanted, what she thought. His dad'd been right that time he'd told him: "If you put the back of your hand across a smart mouth it shuts right up!"

Dennis pressed his fingers against his forehead, drawing his eyebrows closer together, deepening his frown. Shaky, slightly out of breath, he crossed to Rachel's wardrobe. He threw what remained of her clothes onto the bed with the dress she'd worn last night. Then he went downstairs to get a pair of scissors.

"Cunt," he murmured, hacking with cold fury. Beads of sweat dribbled from his top lip. When his breathing became really ragged, Dennis let go the scissors. Looking down he saw his shirt was smeared with blood and recoiled, realising then that only his hand was cut - a slash across the knuckles, a diamond shaped hole just below the middle joint of his little finger.

In the bathroom he ran his hand under cold water before dry-swallowing two Prozac. Before the calmness began to melt through him, Dennis assured himself what he'd done was just a start. He sat on the edge of the bath and let his breathing steady. It'd been a mistake to marry her, but if she thought she was going to walk out on him, just pack the things she wanted and leave, she had another think coming!

## FOURTEEN

Charlie expected them to have a hard time locating Leroy. In fact they went back to Churchill House on the off chance and Leroy was in his flat, at work on a can of cider. Something was different about the place. It took Charlie only a moment to realise the TV had gone. So long as Charlie had known him Leroy'd been a user - the variable being how much he used. No TV meant his habit was on the up. That the TV was gone also meant Leroy was on his own.

"Where's Sandra?" Charlie asked, carefully stepping over the little wall of dust to stand where the TV had been. Waiting for an answer, he looked at Tony Harris - his arms folded, not saying anything, but paying close attention.

"I'm not her keeper," Leroy said. He jammed his hands into his pockets to keep them from twitching.

Three times Charlie had met Sandra. Each time Leroy'd been in trouble and she was doing what she could to help out. She'd started living with Leroy, Sandra'd told him, before he got his habit. A tall, thin woman who worked as a cook in a children's home, she'd looked older each time Charlie'd seen her. She'd left Leroy before. Maybe this time she wasn't coming back. Sandra wasn't why Charlie was here, but thoughts of her distracted him. He looked out the window. Mid afternoon and already it was getting dark. Charlie hated the winter. Louise had left him in the winter. It looked like Sandra'd gone while the snow was on the ground...

Charlie couldn't help connecting things. Then he found himself wondering if Rachel would be there when he got home, and had to work hard to bring his mind back to Leroy and Harry.

"We checked Harry's place," Charlie said. Leroy just looked at him, not really listening, not really taking anything in, his mind already reaching for his next hit. "He wasn't in."

Leroy shrugged.

"People go out."

"He won't be back for some time. But he left a message." That got Leroy's attention. "Two things," Charlie said. "First, I want you to tell us where'd be good to go look for Harry. My guess is he won't have gone far, will still be doing business on the Estate."

Leroy's tongue sneaked out to slide over his lips, like he was getting ready to speak and had a lot to say, all of it denial. But before he could get anything out, Charlie shook his head:

"We don't have time for that stuff. I need you to tell me." He said it quietly, but let Leroy see he meant it. Charlie said: "You can tell us where to go look once you've packed."

"Packed?"

"That's the second thing: You need to get out of here," Charlie said. "In case Harry comes to see you. Remember what we talked about?"

Leroy nodded, though he didn't look sure.

"Will Stan let you stay awhile?"

Leroy blinked. He seemed to be thinking about it. Then he nodded:

"I think so."

"Pack what you need and I'll drive you there."

Charlie followed Leroy's gaze. Only the TV was missing, yet the apartment looked empty - grey and dusty, like it hadn't been lived in for a long time.

"I don't have to pack anything," Leroy said.

Charlie was glad: the quicker they got out of there the better.

## FIFTEEN

"You look tired," Rachel said, and wondered if she was saying too much, talking to Charlie as if he were her husband not her – soon to be ex - brother-in-law. If he'd looked at her harshly, or even paused, she'd have apologised. But it didn't happen that way.

"I am," Charlie admitted. He smiled. Took from her the cup of coffee she held out for him and they sat at the table by the patio doors.

He'd taken off his jacket when he first came in, and still he was too warm.

Seeing that he was looking at her, Rachel said:

"I look tired, too, huh?"

"No." He thought she looked terrific.

"If it's any consolation," she said, smiling, watching him sip coffee, "I actually feel like shit."

For a while they sat in a not uncomfortable silence, seated opposite each other, illuminated by wall lights.

"I brought my things out of the car," Rachel said. "They're upstairs."

"I didn't know if you'd be here when I got back." Charlie paused. He added: "I'm glad you are."

"I didn't know if I'd be here either. I'm glad I am, too."

They looked very directly into each other's eyes, then quickly away, Rachel taking in the boxing trophies on the unit beside the table, Charlie looking out of the patio doors at a black sky and snow-covered white slabs - specifically at the line where black kissed white, wishing his life was as clear cut.

"Are you hungry?" Charlie said, turning to face her again. "I'm hungry."

Somewhere she'd read that people who were really good looking actually looked better when they were slightly ill or a little tired, and in Charlie's case she believed it to be true.

"I got here an hour ago, I should have got something ready."

"If you'd done that, I wouldn't't've got to play the host with the most!"

Charlie rolled up his shirtsleeves.

"You like cheese and tomato pizza?"

"Sounds good."

They ate at the table in the living room, James Taylor on the CD.

"As far as I'm concerned, this is health food," Charlie said, laying down his fork when he'd finished eating.

Rachel smiled. She too had finished eating, but she didn't sit back from the table. James Taylor was singing: *You Got A Friend*. Prompted by this and an instinctive feeling that she was in the right place at the right time, Rachel said:

"You want to hear something funny?"

Charlie nodded. Waited...

"Sitting here with you, now, like this, it's hard for me to believe I was ever married to Dennis at all."

"I wish..." Charlie said - then let it go.

Rachel reached for his hand, but stopped before their fingers met, feeling as if she'd been wakened whilst sleepwalking.

"Will you tell me some things about yourself?"

"When someone says that to me my mind goes blank."

"Let's do it the way they did it in *Silence Of The Lambs* - Clarice and Lecter: Quid pro quo. I tell you something, then you tell me something."

Her cheeks were slightly flushed, as if she'd drunk wine with her food.

"You're saying I'm Hannibal Lecter?"

Charlie liked how easily she laughed. Louise, when he'd tried to make her laugh, always liked to stonewall him.

Rachel said:

"Me first." And told him about her parents' divorce.

"I'll tell you about my dad," Charlie said when it was his turn, working to put the memories into some sort of order. "He was a steelworker," was the beginning he opted for. "I look the way he looked before the booze got hold of him. But he was crazy, and on my good days: I manage to convince myself I'm not." He was glad Rachel smiled at that - it made it easier to continue: "Dad hated himself, I never really knew why. I do know he punished himself. Then he took to punishing my mom. My dad's the reason why, I think, I hate violence."

Charlie saw her eyes lift to the boxing trophies, muscular brass figures on stands. Several times he'd meant to throw them away. Anticipating her question, he voiced it for her:

"Why does someone who hates violence climb into a boxing ring?" And paused only for a moment before giving her his answer: "In the first place, I boxed because dad wanted me to. I was scared of him so I was scared not to do what he wanted me to. Then I found I was pretty useful. And it helped me feel calm inside. Before, I'd always felt tense inside my head. The final thing's harder to explain, but it seemed to make sense to me that me hating violence was all the more reason why I should push myself to...I guess try and master it, learn to be in

40

control of myself around it. I'm telling you all my secrets here," he said. This time when he laughed, she didn't laugh with him. Instead, serious, she said:

"Your secrets are safe with me."

# SIXTEEN

It got dark early, lights coming on all over the Estate. And it'd been a frustrating day in many ways - things not working out how Tony Harris would have liked them to, though they'd got from Leroy the address of one of the guys who worked with Harry. Charlie'd said he'd drop Leroy off at his brother Stan's place and make a fresh start in the morning. "Sure," Harris had said, falling over himself to agree. But as soon as Charlie drove off, Harris had taken out the address he'd copied from Leroy's own address book - a dog-eared thing in which Leroy had spelled everything wrong. It'd been cold and Harris' breath had broken over the sheet of paper with the address on it. If Charlie wants to wait, it's his funeral, Harris'd thought.

43 chanda rowb was what Leroy had written. Harris congratulated himself on being smart enough to translate.

D.S. Harris got out of his car near the cluster of shops at the end of Chandler Road - a video rental store, an off licence, and a Fish & Chip shop. The snow was packed hard and crunched underfoot as he walked from his car to the Fish & Chip shop, the wind blowing the smell of the canal across the backs of the houses.

Inside the shop it was warm, the heat bringing a flush to Harris' cheeks. The smell of fried fish masked the reek of the canal. At a red plastic table near the window, he ate a large portion of chips, cod, and three slices of bread, washing it all down with a can of Coke.

By the time he'd finished eating, it was fully dark, so cold it'd be quiet till the pubs turned out. Harris decided the best way was to rush in. Go straight up to the door and knock. He'd hit Harry first - read him his rights later. Hit him and cuff him and D.I. Harris would become C.I. Harris. The location was different, and the time of day, but essentially what he'd planned that morning Harris intended to make actual now.

When Harris left the shop, the cold felt sharper. But at least now his belly was full. Hit him and cuff him! Keep it simple! Harris closed his eyes and saw it clearly. Slipping in places, he crossed the road to collect Bobby. Then he headed for number 43.

# SEVENTEEN

Harry was pissed off. He knew he'd been right to move, that the coppers would go to his house, knowing it as an instinctive thing - not sure of details like how they'd get the address or when they'd get there - yet knowing it with absolute certainty. But it did feel like the coppers had spooked him into running off. Manraj hadn't said anything, but in Harry's head the words had Manraj's voice: "Harry's been spooked by coppers."

Everyone was in the living room. The curtains were drawn and the heating was on. Harry, Manraj, College and Kerry were all sitting in front of the TV watching kids' programmes. Harry drummed his fingers against the arm of the chair. *Harry's been spooked by coppers.* It kept repeating itself inside Harry's head. Made it impossible for him to concentrate on the TV.

Kerry sat hugging her knees, watching *Scooby Do* like her life depended on it. She wouldn't look at him. His guess was she wanted him to speak first, believing that that'd be tantamount to an apology. Harry shook his head. It'd been just a little slap, nothing serious, and he'd be fucked if he'd apologise for that.

The other times Harry'd been pissed and given Kerry a little slap he'd felt better – it was like taking paracetamol tablets when you had a headache. This time though, it hadn't worked. He went upstairs and rolled a joint, standing by the bedroom window with the light off so he could see out. The snow had made up its mind to be a permanent fixture. A Land Rover crunched by, the guy at the wheel smirking, wanting everybody to see how cool it was having a four-wheel drive in weather like this. Harry sucked on the joint. Giving Kerry a slap was paracetamol, a joint was an antibiotic, but neither was working right now: *Harry's been spooked by coppers!*

Harry smoked and he dreamed. He dreamed the fat copper - the one he'd dropped with a single punch in Churchill House - was on the opposite side of the road, slipping and sliding, pausing to take a sheet of paper from his pocket and look at it.

Only it wasn't a dream. Harry put out his joint. His mind starting to whirr, he used his fingertips to trace the vertical line between his eyebrows. What was this about?

The fat copper stood outside the door of number 43. Knocked the door. Waited. Said something to the old man who answered. The old man shook his head and shrugged: he didn't know anything.

And for the first time since Friday night in Churchill House, Harry started to feel okay. It was clear the fat copper was looking for him; he knew Manraj lived in Chandler Road, but he'd gone to 43 instead of 34!

He smiled as he lifted his jacket from the back of the chair. Cartoon noises still leaking into the hallway, Harry let himself out, zipping his jacket against the cold. Calm, now - no, better than calm: good: alive without being jumpy, tense but not wired, he followed, first on foot, then his car. The last time Harry'd felt this good was when he'd sliced off one of Tommy Morrison's balls.

Harry followed D.I. Tony Harris to the suburbs north of Benbury.

Harris shut off his headlights and got out of his car. That he was disappointed at not finding Harry had made him hungry again, and it was this as much as the cold that drove him to hurry up the driveway.

Harry drove to the end of the street and turned left. Drove to the end of that street and turned right before parking and getting out. He had a way to walk to get to the fat copper's house, but in neighbourhoods like this, they noticed strangers - so it made sense to park and walk.

Harry passed Tony Harris' car, but instead of making for the front door he headed for the garage.

No one was out in the street and, so far as Harry could see, no one was watching from the houses opposite - light from TV screens making patterns across drawn curtains.

Perfect for him.

A ventilator breathed central heating fumes over him. Harry spat away the taste and tried the back gate. It was locked, but Harry climbed it easily, imagining he was Bruce Lee in *Enter The Dragon*.

The back garden, surrounded on three sides by panel fencing, was virgin snow. Harry dropped from the gate, the snow muffling his landing. He liked a joint now and then; and sometimes he'd use a little powder to help iron out the creases, but nothing made him feel as alive as he felt now.

Light from the patio doors painted the snow yellow. Standing in deep shadow, Harry peered into the house. The fat copper and his lady were sitting opposite each other. The TV was on, but they were talking.

Home sweet home!

But not for long…Bruce Lee again, each step fluid and soundless, Harry moved to the back door.

EIGHTEEN

"I can manage," Charlie said.

"I know you can." Rachel picked up the tea towel - souvenir of a visit to Tintagel, a picture of the castle ruins on it. "And if this was a hotel, or if I'd been invited here, it'd be different."

"I invited you."

She smiled. He was kind, and Rachel would have told him so if she hadn't been sure it would embarrass him. "No," she said. "I invited myself and you said I could stay."

"I call that an invitation," Charlie said.

"You call pizza health food," she countered.

Charlie showed her the palms of his hands. Then started in on the washing up.

"You're not like Dennis," Rachel said as she lifted a plate from the drying rack.

"I told you how dad used to hurt mom. What I haven't told you is: I hated him for it. But Dennis..." Charlie frowned. After all these years he still didn't understand it. "...Dennis took it the other way and made up his mind to hate mom. I guess me and Dennis have always been different."

When the washing up was finished, Charlie made more coffee.

"Another thing: I think Dennis hates you."

"Why would he hate me?"

He handed her the coffee. Rachel took a sip. She felt like reaching out and taking his hand in hers. Instead she told him the story Dennis had told her -

- Alan Tombs was seventeen, the oldest of four brothers. His knuckles were big and his eyes were small. He dug holes in his garden to bury the cats he killed, always carrying cat food and a bayonet with him, using the food to attract the cat, then pushing the bayonet through one of its eyes and carrying it home inside the dirty duffel coat he wore winter and summer. During the course of a forceps delivery, his lips had been practically torn off. His speech had always been slurred, though there was nothing wrong with his teeth: he'd been expelled from Manor Comprehensive for biting the Head. Alan Tombs killed cats and he bit headmasters. Nobody knew why; nobody dared ask.

Alan's younger brothers, Michael, Daniel and Aden, still went to Manor Comp. Michael was the same age as Dennis, though the two probably wouldn't have spoken if Dennis hadn't seen Michael stealing a magazine from the newsagent at the end of Manor Road.

*"Tell, and you're dead," Michael hissed. His teeth were yellow and his breath stank. Though he lived on chips, Michael was as skinny as his older brother. Dennis knew about Alan Tombs and his cats. And about their mother, Shirley, who practically lived in The Hay Wain and would suck a man for the price of a gin and lemonade.*

*Dennis wasn't dumb, and his knowledge of the Tombs family would have ensured he kept his mouth shut, turned and walked out of the shop, if Michael hadn't added:*

*"You won't tell - I know you, you're a fucking chicken."*

*His dad thought he was gutless, he knew. When he'd taken his sons to Benbury A.B.A. Bill Grant had seen the oldest demonstrate enough ability to take him into the professional ranks and the youngest shed tears during sparring. Knowing the old man thought it, and hearing Michael Tombs say it, was too much for Dennis...*

*The day after Dennis told on Michael the Tombs brothers came after him.*

*Dennis shouldered his school bag and cut past the headmaster's office to the school field.*

*Reaching it, Dennis turned. What he saw made his heart stutter: all four Tombs brothers were after him.*

*Dennis reached the end of the football field first, but already he was sweating hard and his legs were heavy. He climbed railings separating the field from The Hay Wain.*

*Panic set in when he saw how close Alan was. Half way across the bowling green Dennis tossed away his school bag. If he got through this, he'd have to explain the loss to the old man. But he might not get through it.*

*He climbed a panel fence and crossed the car park. There were no cars, this compounding the feeling that the world was emptying around him, leaving only him...and the Tombs brothers.*

*Dennis kept running, but he was close to exhaustion. He ran past Antonio's Fish & Chips, past Hall's Electrical, both shops run down, their windows filmed with grime. His chest felt like it was ready to burst. He didn't turn round to see if the Tombs brothers were close: he didn't have to: he could feel their presence. Lead-grey clouds pressed down on him. Autumn trees to his left defined the perimeter of the waste ground at the back of Fisher's Fruit & Vegetables.*

*The sound of his own breathing filling his head, Dennis waded through a sea of nettles. The nettles tugged at him. If he'd the breath, he'd have screamed. Instead, he shambled on, almost slipping on fragmented bricks.*

46

The waste ground led to a high, crumbling wall - all that remained of a bottle factory.

There was no way out, Dennis realised too late.

He turned –

And there were the Tombs brothers, Alan in front, sweating, grinning, his foul, meaty breath exploding across Dennis' face.

Alan opened his duffel coat to let Dennis see the bayonet he used to kill cats.

His hands on his knees, his breathing ragged, Dennis glimpsed death, sudden and sharp.

Dennis Grant, fifteen, was found dead on waste ground at the back of shops just a few hundred yards from his school. That would have happened, Dennis was convinced, if Charlie hadn't seen the Tombs brothers chasing him, and followed.

"What's the problem?" Charlie asked, looking and sounding calm.

When he saw Charlie, Alan Tombs reached for the bayonet. His right hand closed around the dark grey hilt and he tugged -

But before the blade came free of its sheath, Charlie hit him - a straight left jab followed by a right cross: textbook stuff.

Looking surprised, Alan let go the bayonet, lurched backwards, then to his left, but didn't go down.

Shifting his weight, Charlie threw a left hook that landed flush on Alan Tomb's jaw. He knew his wrist was broken the moment his shot connected, though there was no sound, just a sudden rush of pain.

If he hadn't compounded the break, his wrist might have healed properly. As it was, Michael Tombs- the spell that had held him in suspension shattered by the sight of his older brother on the floor, suddenly rushed him.

Charlie stunned Michael Tombs with a chopping right hand punch. It stopped his advance. Made him put his arms slightly out to his sides - as if he were about to try and fly.

Aden Tombs dug his right fist into Charlie's kidney and Charlie felt as if his insides had been compacted. He badly needed to piss, but there wasn't time, there wasn't even time to reposition himself so he could hit with his right hand.

Charlie drove his left fist into Aden Tombs' face. The wrist would never be the same again, would for the rest of his life hurt when he subjected it to physical stress, if he were emotionally troubled, and when it was damp or cold.

While Charlie held his shattered left wrist in his right hand, Michael Tombs kicked out viciously, grunting at the point of impact.

(Listening to Rachel telling this story, Charlie remembered his visit to the fertility clinic, the doctor asking him if he'd ever fallen, or been kicked, before going on to explain that damage had been done, damage so severe it couldn't be undone. Charlie had seen his reflection in the lenses of the doctor's glasses. Had watched himself nodding, hating what he'd been told, but feeling as if the final piece of a jigsaw puzzle had been slotted into place.)

*Two of the brothers, Alan and Aden, were on the floor. Michael Tombs, having landed once, got ready to kick out again, intent on putting Charlie down. But Dennis threw himself forwards, teeth gritted, clubbing Michael to the ground with a flurry of punches.*

*The fourth brother, Daniel Tombs, stood with his hands in his pockets, chewing Juicy Fruit at high speed. He didn't move. Didn't say anything even when Dennis put his arm around his older brother's shoulders and helped him through the nettles to the street, the two of them quickly absorbed by the thickening darkness.*

- "You saved him, as a result of which: he hates you," Rachel said. She stood with her lower back against the Formica work surface beneath the kitchen window, both hands wrapped around her empty cup.

It was a little after 10.15PM and Charlie was tired, lack of sleep and a day of running around catching up with him. He wanted to tell Rachel that Dennis' version of what'd happened had a couple of significant holes in it, was working on that when Rachel put down her cup and moved to stand directly in front of him.

"This morning you said you liked me." Looking into his face, she said: "I like you, too." People advised against getting involved on the rebound, but she didn't care.

Rachel had to wait only a moment for Charlie to touch her.

# NINETEEN

December 20th.

At first Kerry thought they were still at Harry's place. It was an easy mistake to make since all the houses on the Estate were alike, square rooms with aluminium window frames that grew beads of condensation as big as button mushrooms. Then she remembered they were staying at Manraj's.

Seeing that Harry was still asleep, lying on his side, making a little clicking noise with his tongue each time he exhaled, Kerry got out of bed, dressing quickly because - this another feature of Estate houses - the place was cold.

Kerry went downstairs, made tea and smoked a cigarette. It was quiet. Outside, it was grey - looked like being one of those days when it didn't get fully light. When she'd drunk her tea, Kerry turned on the oven and stood in front of it, able to think once she was warm.

When Kerry first met Harry, forty-second fucks notwithstanding, he'd been fun. He bought her big bottles of Coco Chanel and a gold ring - showing off. That slowed after a while, but he was still generous and, when he wanted to eat, he wouldn't dream of asking her to fix anything: they always went out. Kerry liked that. As far as using the merchandise was concerned, Harry told her to stay off the H, but the dope was okay so long as she asked him first - pretty please.

It wasn't brilliant, wasn't Kerry's idea of heaven or anything, but living with Harry'd been okay.

Then things had changed: lately Harry'd used her as a punch bag so often Kerry felt entitled to gym fees.

Finished with her cigarette, she fingered her top lip. It was still swollen.

"You want another cup of tea?"

She hadn't heard Manraj come into the kitchen. He smiled. Kerry smiled back at him. She twisted the gold ring Harry'd bought her - the one she wore on the middle finger of her left hand.

"Thinking, yeah?"

"Yeah," Kerry agreed, watching Manraj make tea, skinny compared to Harry, the black jeans and grey tee shirt loose.

# TWENTY

Never one to squander an opportunity to exert power, C.I. Dennis Grant, standing by the side of his Audi, called D.S. Craig over to him.

D.S. Craig, because it had been near the end of her shift when she and D.S. Bishop responded to the alert, looked tired, the skin beneath her eyes grey even in the glare of the ambulance lights.

"Sir?"

"When the media get here," Dennis said, speaking quickly, sharply, "they don't go inside, don't even get to stand in the garden...but don't piss them off. If they're hostile when I make a statement, I'll blame you."

"Sir," D.S. Craig said, feeling the cold even through a heavy overcoat.

Dennis straightened his tie before going into the house, closing the front door after himself.

Immediately he was inside, Dennis smelled blood. Closing his eyes he saw Alan Tombs coming at him with a bayonet, Charlie arriving too late to stop the blade slicing through his school shirt and the soft, white skin of his belly...

When Dennis pushed away this image and opened his eyes D.S. Bishop stepped from the living room to the hall.

"Who else's been inside?"

"Forensics...The ambulance crew...Me...You. "

"The fewer people walk through here, the better." When Dennis was a D.S. himself, a copper had been killed on his patch, a uniformed man with twenty years service, two teenage daughters, and a hysterical wife. The case was tailor-made for the early evening news. Once word was out, it got to be a circus - the crime scene made useless within half an hour, even those who'd hated him when he was alive deciding, now he was dead, that he'd been a terrific copper, one of the best, traipsing through his living room and looking at the framed photographs of his kids to help fire up their indignation, the rest of the world back-seated, nothing like a good murder for doing that. With that case they got lucky - finding out the copper had gambled, and badly: was in debt up to his eyeballs. Two guys he owed had come calling. One of the guys, knowing himself to be inarticulate during times of stress had bought a sawn off shotgun to help if he got tongue-tied - which was what happened. If they hadn't got lucky, though, the case would have stalled, since there were no witnesses and, due to the sightseeing, no crime scene evidence.

With this case, Dennis didn't want to have to rely on luck, was determined to keep the crime scene clean, doing everything by the book. Though of course if they happened to get lucky, and things were wrapped up quickly, he'd gladly soak up the credit

Dennis saw Bishop was ambitious: even in the sparse light leaking from the living room, his eyes were bright and hungry.

"You know this is important?"

"Sir."

"You get first crack."

"Thank you, sir."

"Thank me by getting results."

"I understand, sir."

"Talk me through what you have," he said, following Bishop from the hall to the kitchen, white walls reflecting fluorescent light.

Bishop waited till the C.I. was all the way in.

"Mrs Harris," Bishop said, putting his hands into his pockets to show he was comfortable with what had happened here and what he'd been given to do, "came into the kitchen. The killer was already inside. He heard her coming, went and stood behind the door."

Bishop pointed. There was plenty of space between the door and a fridge-freezer.

"The killer came in through the back door. We found footprints out back - pulled a cast. We'll have more on that later, but judging by the size and depth of the prints, we're looking for a man."

"Go on."

"The killer hears her coming and stands behind the door. She comes in and he grabs her from behind, cuts her throat."

"Nearly cut her head off."

"Which's what makes me think our man's a smack head. If you're a burglar, you don't break a house at this time - everybody's home. If you break in when people are just getting home from work, it's because you're desperate."

When he caught up with her, Dennis intended to tell Rachel about this. Going into detail. Letting her know how easy it was to be hurt...

"So: Mrs Harris is down," Bishop continued. "Now, either: our man didn't make any noise when he did her. Or: D.S. Harris had the TV on in the other room and didn't hear anything."

"Was the TV on when you got here?"

"No." Wanting to show he had all the bases covered, Bishop added: "We'll dust everything, including the remote control."

Dennis nodded. The smell of blood upset his stomach, but he preferred being here to being in his own house, adrift in his anger.

"What's the time of death?"

"After five, before eight is the estimate."

Dennis glanced at his watch. It wasn't yet one, that why the blood smelled so fresh. He blinked. Bit his teeth together - hard - against a wave of nausea.

"Any chance the pizza delivery man who found them, did them?"

"No. He'll be at the station still, but I took a statement as soon as I got here. Bailey's his name. He's fifty-two. He's been delivering pizzas all over the Estate on his moped since he got made redundant from his job as a forklift truck driver. When I got here he didn't have any blood on him. And his right hand's no good: he lost three fingers in an industrial accident. He'd struggle to hold someone with one hand and use a knife with another - be able to do with a single cut what's been done to Mrs Harris. Besides which…he's one of those people who when they lose their job, they shrink. Bailey isn't strong enough to have done it in my opinion."

"What's Bailey actually seen?"

"Mrs Harris had ordered a couple of deep pans - cheese and ham. Bailey got here and rang the bell. There was no answer. Bailey knew it was the right house because he'd delivered here before. They always have the deep pans and Mrs Harris always gives him a tip. The lights were on, so Bailey knew they were in. He rang two or three times, but nobody answered, so he went over to the front window. Bailey says if he takes out a pizza and he can't deliver it, for whatever reason, it comes out of his wages. That's the deal. He was going to tap on the glass. But the curtains weren't shut quite tight. So he looked in. He saw D.S. Harris on the floor. That's when he went for the phone."

"Did he use a neighbour's phone?"

"No. He went to the call box at the end of the street. I asked him why he did that when they've got a phone at the house right next door, and Bailey said the people who live in these houses - money people, he called them - weren't the kind of people you could knock on their door even if it was an emergency."

"So, he called from a pay phone." Dennis nodded to himself, mentally checking things off. "He hasn't spoken to anybody else?"

"No, sir."

"You talked to the pizza man. Did you scare him?"

Bishop hesitated. Wanting to know where the C.I. was going with this.

"He was pretty shaken up already," Bishop said. "It would've been difficult not to."

Bishop crossed his hands in front of his crotch. This was the pose he'd adopted in school photographs. Like a schoolboy was how he was feeling right now. At the station they referred to the C.I. as 'The Shrinking Man.' When Bishop had asked why – he'd been told him it was because when he wanted to the C.I. made you feel two inches tall. This was his first taste of it.

"Good," Dennis said. "When we get through with him at the station, if it turns out he's one hundred per cent and we let him go, I want the pizza man to stay scared - so he doesn't talk to the media, selling gory details to buy a new moped." Dennis looked again at the blood on the floor. A copper had been killed. It was bound to attract the TV and newspapers. If things went well this would be his ticket out of Benbury, but if things got out of hand he was finished.

"So, Mrs Harris is dead in the kitchen, her throat cut from behind." Dennis stepped back from the stain on the floor and scraped his fingertips lightly across his cheeks, as if considering when next he'd need to shave. "What happened with D.S. Harris?"

"This way, sir," Bishop said, stepping neatly past the C.I., glad to be moving again, through to the living room - blue walls, chrome-framed prints. Everything was in its place. Harris had lived a well-ordered life. But now, in the light thrown by a table lamp, Dennis saw the dark stain on the carpet.

"The killer did Mrs Harris in the kitchen then came in here," Bishop said, so low-key he sounded like a bored estate agent. "He still had the knife with him. It looks like D.S. Harris took a look at the killer and backed away. My guess is the killer rushed him. One wound to the chest's all that showed up in the preliminary."

"You do not," Dennis said, raising his voice and jabbing his forefinger at Bishop, "say again what you just said to me. You don't say it to D.S. Craig, or to any other officers. You don't say it to your wife or girlfriend. Not now, not later, not to anyone do you say that one of my officers backed away. Clear?"

"Sir. "

Dennis frowned. What Bishop had said about this being a smack head desperate for money to score made sense…but a smack head wouldn't leave the place so tidy. Think smack head, think chaos.

"What's been stolen?"

"We didn't find wallets, cash, credit cards on either of the bodies - it's pretty safe to assume they were taken."

"I'm outraged," Dennis told the press forty minutes after his meeting with D.S. Bishop, and put that mask on. That a young officer - of "outstanding potential" - and his wife had lost their lives "disgusted" him. He, and all the other officers in Benbury, would do their "utmost" to "apprehend the person or persons responsible for the atrocity."

It was almost 5AM when Dennis finally left Benbury Police Station, wound so tight he was shaking - though it had nothing to do with what'd happened to D.S. Harris and his wife, with facing the press, or with the anxious, already haggard look of all the officers on duty. The case was important, make or break as far as his career was concerned. Yet thoughts of Rachel kept crowding in on him, winding him tighter and tighter.

The roads, freshly gritted, crunched beneath the onslaught of his tyres. Dennis drove very deliberately, not wanting to reach the house.

"It's not that I miss the bitch," he said, as if in response to an accusation. "I don't miss her!" he snapped, and in his mind saw her retreating from him, trying to protect herself with both hands.

# TWENTY-ONE

Charlie slept for little more than two hours, waking suddenly - sure Rachel wouldn't be beside him -

But she was there, and the sight of her, still sleeping soundly, her face turned away from him, made his heart beat fast. He sat up. It was cold. Sometimes, the cold brought with it clarity. But not this time: Charlie couldn't get hold of just what his feelings were.

Moving quietly, he got out of bed, put on his grey sweat suit, splashed water onto his face, then went downstairs and out to the garage to work out.

Hitting the punch bag didn't make anything clearer, but it seemed to relax him. His left hand aside, he was in good shape - the way - if your preparation had gone well - you aimed to be going into a fight. Bag work, then skipping. Afterwards: five rounds of shadow boxing, making his legs move him quickly forwards, backwards, to the left, to the right. To finish, he did sit-ups on the cold concrete floor, staring at the light bulb as he felt his muscles working, fit and disciplined enough to manage twenty-five reps after the pain set in.

Finished, Charlie stretched before going through to the kitchen. He was surprised to see Rachel there, wearing a white towel bathrobe knotted at the waist.

She handed him a mug of tea, wishing she knew a joke, imagining them both laughing and then sipping tea before laughing some more.

The central heating clicked on and radiators began to tick, expanding with the heat.

The panic she'd felt on waking was just starting to subside. It helped that, having scrutinised him closely, she could see Charlie would never - unlike Dennis - ask her how many men she'd slept with.

The first time Charlie saw her Rachel had on a beige skirt three inches short of her knees, and a black pullover. He wanted to tell her he remembered what she'd been wearing - tell her, then, what really happened that afternoon on the waste land with the Tombs brothers and Dennis…

But before he could say anything the phone rang.

It was Frank Connor, calling from the station.

"Have you heard?"

"Heard what?"

Charlie pressed the phone hard against his ear, waiting.

"Tony Harris and his wife have been murdered."

Charlie closed his eyes. Ninth to Ground floor in a second and a half was how his guts felt.

Into an expanding silence, Frank spoke Charlie's name three times before he got a response:

"I'm here." With a concerted effort, Charlie relaxed his grip on the phone. "Tell me what you know," he said.

"It happened last night. Somebody broke into the house and did them both with a knife." A pause. Then: "The C.I. has given the case to Bishop."

"I appreciate you letting me know," Charlie said.

"You'd do the same for me," Frank said. "Charlie? Tell me to mind my own business if you like, but if I was you - I'd stay away from this one." A pause, then: "I know you can't...I just thought..."

"I know."

"Be careful."

When he hung up, Charlie saw Rachel was in the hall with him. That he found it difficult to tell her what'd happened - it was almost a full minute before he was able to speak - he put down to too much time spent alone.

Rachel said when he'd finished:

"Dennis will use this against you. I told you: he hates you. He'll hurt you if he can."

## TWENTY-TWO

Dressed in a charcoal suit with a pale blue shirt and a dark blue tie, Rachel's last sentences still circling inside his skull, Charlie drove to work through snow the colour of exhaust fumes. The sky was ribboned with dark, but the roads were already busy - four shopping days till Christmas and the world and her son out for retail therapy.

When Charlie parked, before he was even fully out of his car, D.S. Bishop came at him.

"Get this straight," Bishop said, "Harris was your partner, but this is my case." He stuck his jaw out aggressively. "You don't interfere, you got that?" Irritated by Charlie's apparent cool, Bishop palmed flecks of spittle from his lips and moved closer.

"Whatever you say," Charlie said.

"I want that promotion. Me. This case, if I do it right, will deliver for me. I'm being honest, right?"

Charlie pocketed his keys. Stood facing Bishop.

"I don't want anybody getting in my way!"

"Okay." Dennis's way, instead of people co-operating with each other for a result, they competed. Charlie sighed. "Whatever you say." It was too cold to stand around. Sure he'd heard all Bishop had to say, Charlie walked.

The scene had played differently inside his head, and the disparity between real and imagined fed Bishop's anger.

"You're taking the piss!" Bishop snapped, and grabbed at Charlie, intending to tell him he should leave the fuck alone.

Watching from her car, a red Renault parked forty yards to the right of the steps, D.S. Janice Craig opened the door. In the eight months they'd been working together, Bishop'd seemed okay until the previous night. Then he'd made up his mind this case was his window of opportunity and monopolised the crime scene till the C.I. got there, after which he'd laid on a display of brown-nosing that'd taken her breath away. Still, Bishop was her partner. She got out of the car, called:

"Bob!"

Hearing his name dissipated his anger. Bob Bishop released Charlie and took a step backwards.

"Remember what I told you," Bob Bishop said, sounding subdued.

If Charlie heard, he didn't show it, climbing the steps without turning around.

Bishop pressed the back of his hand against his forehead. Was surprised when it came away wet. He licked his lips. Tugged restlessly at his tie before walking over to Craig.

"What a prick!" Bishop said.

Craig nodded, once.

"Oh, yeah," she said.

## TWENTY-THREE

It was chaotic inside Benbury Police Station: 8.11AM, 20th December. Uniformed and plainclothes officers hurrying. Telephones ringing. Charlie intended to see Dennis, though how he'd say all he had to say hadn't taken shape in his mind. Still cold from having been detained by Bishop, he was walking quickly, purposefully towards the C.I.'s office when Frank Connor intercepted him:

"Special delivery for you," Frank said, and handed Charlie an A4 manila envelope.

"You okay?"

Charlie took the envelope.

"I'm fine," he said.

"Meaning: you're not, but you don't want to talk about it?"

Charlie nodded.

If Frank hadn't caught up with him, he'd be in the C.I.'s office right about now. But saying what? Hey, brother, point one: what you said about how I work the Estate isn't right: I'm not flashy, but I am solid, and I go after the real bottom feeders; point two: the way you ration promotion, make people work against each other instead of together isn't a good way to do things; point three: Tony Harris was my partner, you should've made it clear to Bob Bishop that I was to be involved with the case - you know I've done homicide work before; point four: you told your wife I dropped two of the Tombs brothers, that time, years ago, when they chased you - which is bullshit ...as is the idea that you dropped one; and by the way, talking about Rachel...

Charlie was glad he was with Frank and not in the C.I.'s office. The time would come when it was right to talk to Dennis, but it hadn't come yet.

He turned the envelope over in his hands. It felt quite bulky. There was no name or address.

"Frank?" He held up the envelope. "How do you know this is for me?"

"I told you - special delivery: A guy came to the front desk and gave it to me. He said it was for you."

"This guy actually said my name?"

"Yeah." Frank nodded. "He said: 'This is for D.S. Grant.' Said you'd know what it was about."

"What did he look like?"

"Young; about five ten; at least a stone heavier than you. He had on a black leather jacket and black jeans."

"Harry…"

Frank loosened his tie.

"Who's Harry?"

"You got a minute?" Charlie asked, and without waiting for an answer led them to his office.

Even with fluorescent lighting, there was so much wood in the small office it seemed dark, funereal. Charlie's desk was nearest the door. The second drawer down still had in it a framed photograph of Louise. When Charlie and Frank entered, no one looked up. The office faced out onto the fire station. Outside, it had started snowing again, big flakes spiralling down from the velvet-grey sky, laying a translucent cover over the dirtied snow.

His heart beating quickly, Charlie looked across the desk at Frank.

"I'm going to need your help," he said. Then he tore open the envelope.

## TWENTY-FOUR

When College had downed his second pint of Black Label he got more talkative.

"When you said Leroy'd shit himself when he saw us, I thought you were joking," College said.

"You know why he was so scared?"

"He thought we were going to cut one of his balls off, same as we did to that guy Tommy."

The slot machine in the corner of the bar of The Blue Dolphin belched out a £20 win. The winner, unshaven, his beer gut hanging out of his jeans, hurried to the bar and handed over part of his winnings for a bottle of Bells, telling the barman - loud, so everybody would hear him - that the whisky was a Christmas present for his wife. When he had it, the winner put the bottle on his table, put *Last Christmas* on the jukebox, then went back to playing the slot machine.

College gulped at his third pint, feeling the effects, lighting up a cigarette to help him think.

"How come we didn't?" College asked.

"Didn't what?"

"Cut one of Leroy's balls off."

"When he gets out of the hospital, after they've fixed his mouth," Harry said, "maybe we will. As long as he's got his habit, he'll always be easy to find."

"Those coppers waiting in Churchill House, was that down to Leroy?"

Harry kept his eyes fixed on his glass. It was still three-quarters full. He didn't want it. After he'd finished with the fat copper and his wife, he'd felt good. Real good! But it'd started to fade. Putting Leroy's teeth down his throat had perked him up again, but it hadn't lasted. Now he was feeling uptight and mention of the other copper just made it worse.

"That's how come Leroy knew the copper's name, right?"

"Right," Harry said. "D.S. Charlie Grant. Mr Cool."

College turned on his barstool. Took in the rest of the bar, crowded this close to Christmas, the place full of smoke. He saw the man who'd won on the slot machine had opened the whisky that was supposed to be his wife's Christmas present, and was pouring some of it into his lager.

Harry pushed his pint towards College, who poured it into his own glass.

"What'll happen," Harry said, "they'll stitch Leroy's face back together and send him home. He'll go back to his flat and when he hears I've put away Mr Cool, he'll think it's over."

"Or he'll think," College said, "you're scared - with all the shit coming from those coppers being done - to do anything else to him."

Harry grinned. He liked that. College had spent a week at Benbury Technical College - then he'd dropped out. It was why they called him College, the irony trowelled on. Really, though, College wasn't especially stupid, wasn't so stupid he didn't see people would expect him to be too scared to move once he'd done both coppers. When that proved not to be the case, Harry would, he believed, be due even more respect. People on the Estate would give him a wide berth. It wouldn't be necessary ever again to remind anybody what kind of man he was.

"Next time we cut off his nut." College blew smoke through the gap in his front teeth.

"Yeah," Harry said. Though first he had Mr Cool to deal with. Harry planned to leave College out of that. Planned to take Manraj along. Manraj'd been on board some time, yet hadn't been involved in anything like this. It was about time, Harry decided, that he saw what - come crunch time - Manraj had in the tank. Harry looked at his watch.

"Come on, Mr Cool," Harry said, his voice almost drowned out by Slade singing: *Merry Xmas Everybody.*

## TWENTY-FIVE

Snow fell for half the day, reasserting its grip on Benbury. By 3PM it was fully dark. Sgt. Frank Connor, his hands in the pockets of a brown overcoat, walked alongside Charlie Grant. It occurred to Charlie that the weather and the way Churchill House smelled were the same as when Tony Harris was still alive. There were chips on the lift floor. A crushed beer can.

The ninth floor was in almost total darkness, just as it had been two days ago.
 Working in the station Frank had forgotten how places like this smelled, was glad to be out of the lift, though it wasn't much better here.
"You okay?"
"That's my line," Frank said. He smiled as the lift doors rattled closed, leaving them stranded.

The door to Leroy 's flat was ajar. Charlie led them in.
Smelling of fries and fish fingers, still in her red work apron, Sandra Kleestow, tall like Leroy, thin like Leroy, but - unlike Leroy - with eyes that were sharp and clear, sat on the arm of the settee. Though she looked worn out, seeing it was Charlie, Sandra smiled.
"I'm sorry."
"You've always looked out for Leroy. If I didn't know that, I wouldn't've called you."
"Is he alright?"
"He's asleep." Sandra nodded towards the bedroom door. Breathed out so fully her whole upper body seemed to diminish. "But is he alright? Well, he's not dead..."
Charlie blinked. The backs of his knees ached - as if he'd been standing for hours. "I thought he'd be okay with Stan."
"They can only stand each other in small doses." Sandra smiled to herself, as at some private joke - funny, but cruelly so. "Leroy rang my mom last night to say he was staying with Stan. He told her he was keeping out of harm's way. Getting clean."
"That was the idea," Charlie said. He'd had toast for breakfast, nothing since, and it was starting to tell, his hunger accentuating the tiredness he felt. Leroy was supposed to be safe with Stanley. But it hadn't worked out that way...

Charlie'd emptied onto his desk the contents of the envelope Harry had delivered to the station. The envelope contained: a wallet, with a dark stain in one corner. Charlie had used the tip of a pen to open it.

Tony Harris' wallet contained three credit cards and a photograph of Tony and Allison Harris on holiday, the sea in the background a shimmering blue. Dressed in matching yellow tee shirts and shorts, Tony and Allison Harris smiled at the camera, brave and hearty for their posterity.

Gathering himself, Charlie'd continued his examination of the wallet, Frank moving closer so he could see everything.

"What the fuck's this about?"

Charlie believed Harry had killed Tony and Allison Harris, though the wallet on its own, even if they found Harry's prints on it, wouldn't stand up. He needed to find Harry, and ask him: "Did you do it? Did you kill D.S. Harris and his wife?" He had an idea Harry'd admit it because he believed Harry was out to prove something, and a confession plus prints would put Harry away.

Cop movies where the maverick cop doesn't involve anyone else - preferring to Go It Alone - always pissed Charlie off. His whole career, Charlie had played the team game. But he hadn't wanted to hand over the wallet and what he knew. Instead he'd decided to have the wallet printed. Then, with Frank's help, to take twenty-four hours to try and find Harry his own way, combing the Estate carefully, going to the places users met dealers, checking out the address he'd got from Leroy. Twenty-four hours, after which if they could find no sign of Harry, he'd hand over all he had. He'd told Frank if need be he'd tell everyone he'd twisted his arm to come along - this to protect Frank if Dennis decided to take scalps. (Which Dennis would do if, as Rachel had suggested, Dennis hated him.)

They'd been ready to leave the station when Stanley Blackstock called and told him Leroy'd gone.

Instead of searching for Harry, they'd spent hours looking for Leroy, getting nowhere until Sandra rang him.

"Getting clean," Sandra repeated, staring at the space where the TV had been. "If I had a fiver for every time Leroy told me he was getting himself clean, I wouldn't need to play the Lottery."

"What happened?" Charlie asked.

Sandra said:

"He was at Stan's. He'd been there since you dropped him off. Maybe they had words." She shrugged. "I don't know. Maybe Leroy just got itchy. Anyway, he went out to buy." Sandra sighed, resigned to, but still saddened by, Leroy's habit. "He knew it was dangerous. But he went back to the Estate." Another smile flitted across Sandra's face. "He went fishing and the game keeper came."

"Harry?"

Sandra nodded.

"And College: Harry wants people on the Estate to be scared of him, but he likes to have backup." She blinked. "It happened on the car park of The Highwayman on Barlow Street."

Charlie nodded. He knew the place - one of half a dozen pubs on the Estate where users could buy.

"They hurt him, then they ran away." She didn't want to cry. Already she'd cried too many tears for Leroy and she knew her tears wouldn't help him. "When I left I told him he wasn't to ring me any more, not even when he was in trouble. But he did. Leroy and habits, eh!" The smile again, then: "He rang me at work. As soon as I saw him I knew he'd have to be stitched. I drove to A & E. He needed someone to bring him home. I brought him home. Then I rang you."

"You're not staying?" There was no accusation in Charlie's voice.

Sandra pressed her lips together and shook her head. "I'll sleep on the settee tonight, make sure he's okay, but when he wakes up in the morning, I'll go. Being with Leroy - its no life at all.

"Mr Grant," Sandra said, standing up, "Harry and College asked Leroy about you - your name and where you live."

Charlie's eyes were sore. His nerves were starting to fray. It was difficult to keep the edge from his voice when he asked:

"Did Leroy tell them?"

His old man, full of cider at the time, had told Charlie he was too soft. He saw it in him, the old man said. In the ring he won, but he lacked killer instinct. The old man had liked his clichés, but he was right - Charlie did have a soft spot, he could be reached. Which was why a year ago, when Leroy was trying to get clean and his brother was helping out, Charlie'd said to get in touch if he could help.

His stomach fluttered. The past, Charlie saw, could reach into the present at any time.

"Leroy doesn't know where you live," Sandra said.

And for a second Charlie felt relief.

But only for a second...

Leroy didn't know where Charlie lived, but Stan did - Harry'd be able to get to him through Stan.

"Did Harry ask Leroy where he'd been staying?"

Sandra tried to remember everything Leroy had said - able to see from Charlie's face this was important. She turned on the light and all three squinted against the sudden brightness. The dust swirled in slow motion.

"I don't know."

"That's okay," Charlie said, knowing he had to see Stan - to make sure. The darkness and the snow would conspire to slow them. It was important to hurry, yet Charlie took a moment to say goodbye to Sandra, and to wish her luck.

## TWENTY-SIX

When you worked in an office the trick was to take your lunch break as late as possible; then, with most of the working day under your belt, the afternoon seemed to pass quickly. At 1.30PM, Rachel shut down her computer. Margaret and Saida looked across at her. It was to be expected: she'd told them she'd left her husband and they'd taken to studying her. There were grey rings under her eyes, but Rachel smiled at her colleagues as she eased from her workstation.

The air inside the building society had a metallic taste to it and Rachel was glad to get out into the cold until she saw Dennis' car. In another life she'd tried and failed to explain things to him. She didn't intend to try again. Nor did she intend to let herself be bullied, which was just as well.

"Get in!" he snapped.

"Am I under arrest?" she asked.

There were four shopping days left till Christmas and the streets of Benbury were crowded, people with armloads of packages wading through slush.

Rachel saw in his eyes: cold fury. She knew he wanted to force her into his car, but the thought of what that might do to his precious career held him back.

Husband and wife glared at each other - for a moment transfixed.

Then Rachel stepped into the road. An icy gust yanked open her jacket, but that wasn't why she was shaking.

"We're finished," she said.

The crowds seemed to diminish his strength. Dennis laid his hands on the trim, squinting against the wind. She was a lucky woman – there were too many people around to do anything! He consoled himself with the knowledge that it wouldn't always be so – her luck wouldn't last.

"I'm staying with your brother. My solicitor will be in touch."

With that she let herself drift with the flow of people pressing past her. Not until she reached the fountain at the centre of the town – the water in it frozen, a dead robin atop the ice, its entrails unpacked on the glistening surface - did Rachel turn. Expecting to see Dennis, she scanned the nearby faces, her heartbeat rapid and hard…

But Dennis wasn't there.

It's over, Rachel told herself, little knowing…

## TWENTY-SEVEN

Harry pulled over to let College out of the car. The houses on this part of the Estate had been refurbished just ten months ago, but the materials and work were inferior and already the street looked little different to the rest of the Estate.

"Get out."

College did, and weaved up the path to his front door, patting his pockets to find a cigarette.

Harry drove quickly away. Everything except confronting the cool copper – Mr Cool – had become unimportant to him. He put on a CD. It didn't help. Instead he lucked onto the news. Listened to the report about the double homicide in Benbury. When he met up with Mr Cool, Harry intended to taunt him about what he'd done. He'd tell Mr Cool how his partner had backed away from him, begging. He'd enjoy watching Mr Cool heat up, like milk in a pan. He'd keep the gas on till it bubbled right over. Once Harry saw fear in Mr Cool's eyes he'd stop feeling so keyed up, he was sure.

First, he'd get something to eat. Then he'd watch *Enter The Dragon* and have a smoke. He'd sleep for a couple of hours before going to see Leroy's brother, Stan. He'd cut Stan just a little bit – telling him it was a tattoo – that the ladies would like it, which'd crack even Manraj's face. From Stan Harry'd get Mr Cool's address. Then they'd pay him a visit: a night call. If his wife was there, he'd make Mr Cool watch while he cut her, wanting Mr Cool to know the same was going to happen to him.

Harry had everything planned, but when he got back to Manraj's house there was no one there.

Harry called their names from the bottom of the stairs. The quiet had a quality he imagined he could feel against his skin. It was late afternoon and almost dark in the hallway. He heard a clock in one of the bedrooms ticking off the seconds as he climbed the stairs.

Kerry'd gone out to get a take-away and Manraj was getting cigarettes, Harry told himself.

But in the back bedroom drawers had been emptied and the wardrobe doors were open.

It was the same with the front bedroom, yet for several minutes - marked by the clock, the ticks louder up here than on the stairs - Harry persisted in seeing them in shops: Kerry paying for the take-away, Manraj carrying cigarettes.

Kerry and Manraj had gone...

Harry shook his head in disbelief, a disbelief that intensified when, on hands and knees, he reached into the dusty darkness beneath the bed and found the green sports bags full of gear were gone, too.

He stood up. For several seconds Harry held his anger inside. Then it came pouring out, hot as lava. He threw punches at the wardrobe doors until the skin peeled from the knuckles of both hands, then staggered backwards and sagged onto the bed. If they thought he'd let this go, they were mistaken! He'd put out the word! Do what was necessary to find them. Kerry and Manraj were as good as dead! Harry watched blood flowing through his fingertips.

"You're fucking dead!" he said, biting the words off.

But first…

Harry went through to the bathroom and ran his hands under cold water, the torn skin dancing in the flow – red then white.

Kerry and Manraj were dead, but first he'd deal with Mr Cool, first he'd get that out of the way.

In fact he'd go do it right now!

Coming to get you Mr Cool, Harry thought. His hands hurt. The pain helped him stay calm as he zipped up his jacket and left the house.

Already the streetlights were winking on.

"Coming to get you," Harry whispered, turning the key and punching down the gas.

## TWENTY-EIGHT

After seeing Rachel outside the building society in the town centre, Dennis returned to the station to give two smooth, polished interviews on the double murder. That done he closed his office door, took the phone off the hook, sat down. His mouth tasted as if he'd been in a deep sleep. She was staying with his brother was what she'd said. Rachel and Charlie…Charlie and Rachel…Dennis pictured them saying his name and laughing, still sticky-wet from fucking.

He remembered the old man laughing at him, too. The old man had taken him and Charlie to Benbury A.B.A. He wanted to make men of them, he said, winking at George, who ran the club, a pro in the Fifties with a cauliflower ear and thick scar tissue above his eyebrows to prove it.

George picked out two of his lads for them to spar with. Charlie, being the eldest, went first. The smell of leather, old sweat and liniment combined. The boy came at Charlie. He was practiced and sure of himself. But Charlie made him look clumsy, circling, throwing punches when the boy moved in on him. "He's a good lad," George said.

Dennis was next. He faced a stocky, freckle-faced boy and, desperate to do well after Charlie's example, rushed in.

He didn't see the punch coming, didn't feel any pain, remembered only the gritty feel of canvas against his knees and the bitter, coppery taste of the blood smeared across his teeth. He looked across at the old man, wanting approval - at least he'd tried…But the old man only laughed, the laughter more than the blood or the humiliation bringing on the tears.

Dennis blinked away the memory. Put the phone back on the hook and worked for three hours, though thoughts of Charlie and Rachel were never far from his mind.

Driving away from the station, his face felt numb. The darkness rushed at him. Rachel had always wanted him to tell her more about his early life. He'd refused. But now, now Dennis had made up his mind to tell her all about the old man. He'd show her how the old man had acted, see how she liked that…

70

TWENTY-NINE

"If I drink that I'll be sick!"

"I want you to be sick!" Harry snapped.

College swallowed more black coffee followed by salt then – obligingly – he coughed, spluttered, and sprayed vomit into the kitchen sink: over plates and bowls ready to be washed up.

Harry retreated from the smell, overpowering in the tiled kitchen.

College wiped his mouth with the back of his hand. Pale, he held onto the sink unit for support.

"I'm okay," he said, though Harry hadn't asked.

"Get your jacket," Harry said, handing College a lighted cigarette. The kitchen shadows sharpened his features – made him look angrier than ever. In three pulls he smoked his own cigarette down to the filter. "Hurry up," he said, and College nodded, though his speed didn't increase.

"Where we going?" College asked, following Harry out of the house and along the snow-covered path to the car.

"Are we going to cut Leroy's balls off after all?" he asked, seeing two brand new Stanley knives on the back seat.

"We're going to see Leroy's brother: Stan. When I've talked to him we're going to see Mr Cool. Now shut the fuck up and get in!"

A cat darted from the pavement and Harry swerved to hit it, but the cat was too quick and for several minutes they drove in silence, weaving their way through the Estate.

Looking across at him, College saw Harry had that crazy look in his eyes again. More than all the black coffee he'd drunk, it sobered him.

"We're going to settle a couple of scores - the first one tonight," Harry said, speaking quietly, as if sharing a confidence.

Snow was piled high on both sides of the road. It was like driving through a canyon.

"All the time you've worked for me," Harry said, glancing across at College, "you've never tried to fuck me about." He grinned. "When both the scores are settled I'm going to see you get a car like this one. You like the sound of that?"

"Damn right I do," College said, and despite the craziness in College's eyes he started to relax.

THIRTY

Walking back to work, the cold stinging her lips and tearing her eyes, Rachel was convinced she was really free of Dennis and felt good about it, but re-entering the building society, the sudden change of temperature - from icy cold to stifling warm - left her disoriented.

As soon as she re-opened her station a man stood before her, mumbling, his mouth pinched and hostile. She took his passbook and completed the transaction, though her computer seemed to dawdle.

Throughout the afternoon Rachel's fingers dealt with the next customer and the next. The disorientation she felt didn't dissipate. In just a few days a lot had happened and it was catching up with her. Time dragged. She was tempted to shut down her computer and walk away, but she toughed it out till closing time, feeling as if this proved something.

When she'd worked through her totals, Rachel tidied her workstation and shut down the terminal. Her head felt as if the blood vessels had shrunk, the pressure of blood through her eyes painful. Passing the branch manager's desk she saw two bundles of £50 notes. It was policy to ensure cash was never left out, but this close to Christmas mistakes were made. Rachel scanned the branch. The other women were still shutting down their terminals, clearing their workstations, and the branch manager, Mrs Whitby, four months after a double mastectomy, was searching for a lost contact lens.

Almost without thinking, Rachel pocketed the bundles of money and kept walking.

"Good night," Mrs Whitby said.

"Good night," Rachel said, waving to Margaret and Saida as she opened the door to leave.

Stepping outside was like diving into seawater, and she gasped. For a second she stood rooted to the spot. The Christmas lights looked blurry. Rachel slid her hand into her pocket and gripped the bundles of money. She should turn around right now and return them, she knew. But instead she walked away, her head down.

## THIRTY-ONE

Charlie drove quickly through the Estate, the darkness accentuating the twinkle of Christmas lights.

"This's is all tied together, right?" Frank asked.

Charlie was glad Frank was with him. Frank was solid. Gutsy.

"I'm pretty sure I know who killed Tony and Allison Harris," Charlie said.

"The guy who bought the envelope in."

"Yeah."

Charlie told Frank everything - how he and Harris had missed Harry in Churchill House. How Harry had left him a knife on his front doorstep.

"First a knife, then the envelope. He's got a thing about you."

His eyes on the road, Charlie nodded.

"Maybe you ought to turn over what you have."

"I need to make sure Leroy's brother's alright - that Harry, trying to get to me, hasn't got to Stan. Tomorrow, Dennis can have it all."

Frank nodded. Everything was happening too quickly. Always, with this kind of thing, it was the same.

"Here we go," Charlie said. He killed the engine and shut off the headlights. Then he gripped his left wrist in his right hand, squeezing the sudden pain.

"The snow makes everything quiet. Even me," Frank noted, for he was whispering.

His eyes on Stan's house, Charlie said:

"I'll go in."

"Five minutes?" Frank asked.

Nodding, Charlie moved away from the car. If he didn't return in five minutes, there was a problem and Frank'd call for backup.

There was no front gate. Charlie stepped between the posts marking where it had been. The house was quiet. Near the front door it seemed especially dark. There was a familiar dryness inside his mouth. He hoped Harry hadn't been here already - then he could persuade Stan to pack a few things and go to stay with a friend for a few days, just to be on the safe side.

But as he reached out to knock, Charlie saw the door was ajar. The hammering inside his chest intensified as he reached out...

Charlie pushed the front door all the way open...

Then he stepped inside...

## THIRTY-TWO

Twenty minutes before Charlie arrived, when Stanley Blackstock opened his front door, Stan tired after a ten-hour shift, Harry grinned - then butted him.

Overanxious, Harry mistimed the butt - he cracked two of Stan's lower front teeth, but at the same time opened a two-inch gash in his forehead. Blood ran freely into his eyes, and as Harry wiped at it with his sleeve Stan, hurt but not floored, ran along the short, carpet-less hallway and up the stairs, his work boots clattering on the wood.

College, behind him, remained stationary until Harry yelled at him:

"Get the fucker!"

College gave chase but – the alcohol still in him – fell halfway up the stairs, winding himself.

Harry came in and closed the front door. The muscles in his jaw clenching, he passed College. The bathroom was at the top of the stairs. Stan had locked himself in. Harry sighed. Pressing his left hand against the cut to staunch the flow of blood, he leaned close to the bathroom door, his face just an inch from a tile with the outline of a figure on the toilet, lines of strain emanating from its face.

"You're a fast runner," Harry said. His voice echoed as if he were in a grotto. He placed his right hand against the door and listened.

Stan, his back against the toilet, booted feet braced against the door, breathed shallowly to avoid making noise. Leroy had told him about these guys. He couldn't remember their names, but he did remember Leroy saying they were bad news. You got that right, little bother! Stan decided.

"I can bust the door down," College said, beside Harry on the landing, now, wanting to make amends for having fallen.

Ignoring him, Harry addressed the door again:

"My man here wants to break down your door. It's how he keeps fit. Me, I'm not like that. I'm a civilised guy. Last election, if I'd voted, I'd've voted Conservative. I know doors cost money. I don't want to break down your door unless we have to." He studied his hand. The knuckles were caked with blood. His fingers were starting to stiffen. Working hard to contain his anger, he said: "This is about choice. Choice one – you tell me what I want to know and we piss off…Choice two – you keep saying nothing and we break down the door and kick the fuck out of you." When he flexed his fingers, plasma squeezed through the newly formed scabs. "All I want is a copper's address - where does D. S. Grant live?"

74

The cnamel had chilled his back, and his feet were numb. Stan was scared and he felt ridiculous. He burped – softly – tasting again the meatball sandwich he'd eaten for lunch. D.S. Grant had done his best to help Leroy. It hadn't worked out, but he'd gone out of his way to do what he could. Stan liked D.S. Grant, and if he could have come up with a way not to tell, he would have. But nothing came to mind. The bathroom window was too small for him to climb through. There was nothing he could use as a weapon. If he didn't tell them what they wanted to know, they'd come for him. Seeing no way to avoid it, Stan cleared his throat and gave them D.S. Grant's address.

Harry was glad College was here to witness how scared Stan sounded.

"You're smarter than your brother, you know that?"

Stan liked to think he was smarter than Leroy. Yet it troubled him that, if he was smart, he could be in such a fix. The cold had spread from his back. He wedged his hands between his thighs to keep them warm, listening to the footsteps on the stairs. The two men were like elephants. The whole house shook. Stan narrowed his eyes. It occurred to him the men were making all that noise because they wanted to convince him they were going, when in fact they were downstairs, waiting for him to come out…Stan made up his mind to wait fifteen minutes before he opened the door, the only trouble being: he didn't have his watch with him. After calculating for a moment, Stan began to count - slowly - inside his head. When he got to 900 he'd unlock the bathroom door and go downstairs.

He'd reached 812 when he heard footsteps on the stairs, these lighter: not an elephant: a panther. He'd been right to wait. Shivering with cold and fear, Stan pressed his chin to his chest. He was ready for their entry. Ready for the beating…

But the voice that called his name belonged to D.S. Grant.

# THIRTY-THREE

Rachel parked outside Charlie's house, took the stolen money from her pocket and laid it on the passenger seat. It was dark. She was cold. She reached into her purse to take out the key. Her hand wasn't steady. That didn't surprise her: she'd left her husband; begun a relationship with his older brother; had stolen money from work; and to top everything off, she was now ravenously hungry. The hunger it was that propelled her out of her car and to the house.

The house was warm and Rachel was glad of it. She went through to the kitchen. She hated to cook and did it badly, yet it felt good to peel potatoes and chop carrots. Her hands grew steady. Taking the money had been stupid. What had she been thinking? Yet – perhaps absurdly - she was convinced things were looking up. Carrots, potatoes, peas, chicken. With it they needed some wine. She checked the fridge. It was empty. Deciding to get a bottle from the All-Night shop just around the corner, she put her jacket back on. Rachel was feeling good despite everything until she opened the front door and saw Dennis.

He pushed her, not so hard she'd fall over, but hard enough to make her take a step backwards.

Dennis liked the look of surprise on her face. Was she surprised to see him? Or surprised he'd pushed her?

By the time she'd regained her balance, Dennis was in the hall with her.

"Are you stupid?" she demanded.

Dennis grinned, the skin around his hurtful eyes creasing like parchment.

"You must think so."

She felt her heart juddering and caught the odour of her own sweat. It smelled of fear.

Dennis felt the blood pulsing through his lips and cheeks, swelling his fingers.

"Did you really think I'd let you make a fool of me?" He angled his head. It was a move he'd copied from a teacher he'd hated. He laughed. It sounded harsh as a rusty can scraped across concrete. "You look like shit," he said. Clearly it pleased him. "You tried to make me look bad," he said. "If I just let that happen…if I did nothing, I might as well put a gun to my eye. " Dennis placed his right index finger against his right eye and cocked his thumb. A lot of would be suicides - he knew - put the gun in their mouth. Then the bullet went through the roof of their mouth, ricocheted around inside the skull, was deflected and hit the spine, the result paralysis, not suicide. Through the eye was better. Surer.

Dennis took a step forwards. Lowered his hand. Little beads of sweat stood out on his forehead and top lip, the light above him picking them out.

"I'm better than Charlie," he said. He wasn't grinning anymore. "Did you think you'd say a few words to me on a crowded street and I'd run away? Did you think it'd be that easy?"

"Easy?" She'd glimpsed the nastiness in him before, but it'd always been held in check. Now his mask was gone and the real Dennis Grant, poisoned by his past, was bearing down on her. "You think things have been easy for me?" Her throat felt raw. "I didn't leave you…you drove me away." His presence left a bad taste in her mouth – like blood from an abscess. "You didn't ever love me. You don't love yourself, so how can you love anybody else?"

"Shut up!" He thought he sounded different - sounded like the old man. Frowning, Dennis half turned to study the wallpaper – creamy whirls rising from floor to ceiling - and exhaled, his temples throbbing.

Then he hit her.

She went over like a skittle, her cheek swelling immediately, and, his eyes over-bright, Dennis moved in on her.

"I couldn't let you go and do nothing," he hissed.

Rachel knew she was in trouble. She struggled into a sitting position, her feet on the bottom stair. Dennis was so close she could smell his breath – a sickly, cloying sweetness that turned her stomach.

Pleased with himself, Dennis straightened up and started laughing. He hadn't laughed so hard in years. Maybe never. The sound of his laughter obscured the sound of Harry and College moving through the living room to reach the hall…

# THIRTY-FOUR

Cold sweat dribbled down his cheeks. Stay calm, he told himself, but when he saw the grit lorry, panic flared in his chest. The darkness had solidified. A strobic light illuminated the efforts of two workmen in reflective clothing. Breath pluming from their mouths, the workmen attacked the spilled grit with shovels.

Charlie stopped the car, the tyres scrunching snow, and turned it round. The alternative route would add five minutes to the journey. It wasn't much, but he knew it could make all the difference. He had a bad feeling about all this.

"Stan had no choice," Charlie said. Frank noted the urgency in his voice. But he didn't say anything. "He did the right thing," Charlie said.

"Harry knows where you live?"

Nodding, Charlie cornered the way he'd been taught: slow in, fast out, accelerating past the dairy – a picture of a cow illuminated by a night light in front of the main entrance.

"So: Harry goes to your house. You're not home – what's the problem?"

"Rachel might be there," Charlie answered, his voice low, his eyes fixed on the road ahead, trying to dismiss both the sensation that the streets were narrowing, and his memory of the crime scene photographs of Allison Harris. Talking to keep his thoughts at bay, he added: "She'd left Dennis and she needed somewhere to stay." He hoped she wasn't there. That she'd gone shopping, to the cinema, was sitting drinking coffee with a friend, anywhere safe...

Now they were nearly there and his heart felt like it was coming out of his chest.

"Call in," Charlie said.

Seeing the BMW parked opposite the Hawthorns School Charlie guessed it belonged to Harry. He had, he realised, been expecting to run into Harry sometime very soon.

Charlie hadn't, though, expected to see the Audi parked behind Rachel's car. *Dennis...*

He winced. The pain in his wrist intensified and his balls started to ache. He parked and cut the engine. Fear boiled inside his chest.

"Stay here," Charlie said, moving quickly towards the house.

# THIRTY-FIVE

College was hung over. His mouth tasted sour and his temples throbbed insistently. Feeling lousy made him angry. Here, College hoped to use some of his anger. Holding a knife in one hand, he used his free hand to push open the door to the hallway.

The woman at the bottom of the stairs would have seen him, but her eyes were shut. The big man would have seen him, but his back was turned. Neither of them heard him because they were busy with their own thing, first arguing, then laughing, the sound filling the house.

"Merry Christmas," College said, and when the big man turned – slowly, the way a lot of big men moved – College cut him...

THIRTY-SIX

Charlie let himself in through the front door. The hallway was in darkness. His stomach palpitating, he stepped into the living room. It was dark in there, too, but the curtains were thin and let in a fuzzy orange light from the street.

"Mr Cool." Harry sounded pleased with himself. Poised. Ready.

Charlie stood still. This, he knew, was like defusing a bomb - if you made the wrong move, you blew yourself up. Rachel was in the armchair by the fire, still as a Victorian photograph. From where he was standing Charlie couldn't see the details of her face – just a vague, orange smudge, as if she were wearing a mask. Harry lit a cigarette and Charlie glimpsed Dennis, sitting next to the TV, College beside him - a Stanley knife like the one left on Harry's front doorstep in College's hand.

In the moment before the lighter was extinguished, Charlie saw the collar of his brother's shirt was dark-stained.

"I hope I didn't keep you waiting," Charlie said, keeping out of his voice what the stain on Dennis' shirt made him feel.

Harry's cigarette glowed. Through the red glow his right hand moved – slowly, as if he were trying to close the distance on a fly – and sucked a Stanley knife from his jacket pocket.

Two men in leather jackets, each with a Stanley knife. Charlie focused on them. He said:

"Once you stopped running I found you easy."

"Running?" Harry tried to make light of it, but didn't pull it off. "You hear this guy?"

"I hear him," College acknowledged.

"Is he fucking cool or what?"

"He's pretty cool," College conceded.

"How long do you think he'll stay cool when we start carving?"

"Not too long."

"Is that right?" Charlie asked – keeping things easy sounding. By now back up was on its way. However things turned out, Harry and College wouldn't walk away from this. But it wasn't enough to stall them till the back up arrived: Charlie knew Harry wasn't the type to be talked out - couldn't live with himself if he lost face. It wasn't enough to stall - Charlie knew he had to draw Harry and College away from Rachel and Dennis. "Is that right?" he repeated, letting scorn creep into his voice.

"I think so," Harry said. "We'll start with your wife."

80

"She isn't my wife," Charlie said. He was glad it was too dark to see Rachel's face. "Was that your plan? You planned to use my wife to put the squeeze on me?" Charlie faked a laugh. It came out pretty good considering. "Harry…" Charlie tutted.

Finished with his cigarette, Harry dropped it onto the carpet. He squeezed the Stanley knife so hard the grip left its imprint on his fingers. This wasn't going the way he wanted it to go. He felt jumpy. That the woman wasn't D.S. Grant's wife made sense: She was connected in some way to the fat guy. That was why they'd been arguing. Harry knew he'd been careless - he should have found out who the woman and the fat guy were right away. Instead, he'd made an assumption and the assumption had turned out to be a mistake. Harry felt his mistakes were ganging up on him. The deal in Churchill House…Manraj and Kerry…Now this! Harry felt bad. And the way D.S. Grant spoke to him - as calm as if he were ordering a burger and fries at McDonald's - made him feel worse.

"I'm disappointed in you," Charlie said. His heart beat so hard he felt it would break through his ribs. "But I shouldn't be. The truth is you're scared of me." His left foot was fifteen inches in front of his right foot, his weight evenly distributed. "Did he tell you," Charlie began, addressing College now but keeping his eyes on Harry, sure Harry was the driver, College the passenger, "he ran away from me? I told him to run, and he ran." Charlie felt the tension in Harry. Knew he had to prod him just a little more and he'd come at him, leaving Rachel. He was about to force out another laugh, certain it would secure Harry's charge...

Dennis chose that moment to make his move.

## THIRTY-SEVEN

From the base of his neck to a point midway down the right side of his back Dennis was cut – and could feel his shirt clinging to his flesh. He hadn't moved since Charlie came in. Had sat thinking about the old man. In his prime the old man always looked like he needed a shave. Dark hair. Sharp features. Could drink half a dozen pints of Brew XI in an hour. Charlie hadn't ever told him what'd happened with the Tombs brothers, but somehow the old man had known. "You're gutless," the old man had said to Dennis, and his words had hurt more than anything before or since, hurt because Dennis believed them to be the truth, hurt because he was desperate for the old man's approval.

The lack of it had left a hole in him - a hole Dennis had spent much of his life trying to fill. Was trying to fill still...

Dennis couldn't wait for Charlie to save him, not again – not this time. He made up his mind: This time *he* had to do something -

He grabbed at College.

Dennis was big enough and strong enough. If he'd managed to get hold of College, he'd have survived.

But Dennis was too slow. College saw him start his move and reacted, driving the blade of his knife fiercely across Dennis' throat, releasing a dark rope of blood.

## THIRTY-EIGHT

As Dennis sagged forwards, Harry launched himself at Charlie, and Rachel stood up.

Dennis had come here to hurt her, and he'd succeeded – with his words and with his hands. He'd hurt her and she hated him, but she didn't want this to happen, not this. Rachel's lips moved, desperate to say his name. But no sound escaped her throat.

Charlie watched Dennis's hands climb to his throat. Blood ran through his fingers and his eyes bulged. Save me, brother, please save me! Charlie felt rather than heard the words, and he did try - though words spoken and unspoken flowed between them like a poisoned river, he did try, reaching College before Harry got to him, before he could cut Dennis again.

College slashed at Charlie with the knife.

Compared to Dennis, College was fast, but compared to Charlie he was a man wading through mud. Charlie swayed backwards, letting the blade hiss past him. Then he threw a perfectly timed, perfectly executed right hook that landed flush on College's chin, and like a hinge College folded in on himself, his pupils exploded, his lips slack.

Sucking in air, Charlie moved past College to get to Dennis.

But Harry was finally on him.

He felt the blade - white-hot - rush from his left shoulder blade to the right side of his waist. If Charlie hadn't been moving towards Dennis, it would have gone deeper.

Turning, he took the second slash across his right shoulder, the pain racing along his arm, a forest fire.

But pushing the pain from his mind, Charlie opened Harry's cheek to the bone with a right cross.

It was a good punch, but Charlie had over-committed himself, momentum pulling him off balance, leaving him exposed. It could have been over, then, but Charlie got lucky on two counts: First: Being hit enraged Harry and, his bloodied face contorted by rage, he slashed wildly, missing Charlie completely the first time, scoring the underside of his forearm the second. Second: Rachel hit Harry as hard as she could: driving both her fists into the back of his neck.

Charlie was hurt. He was bleeding heavily, but seeing his chance he went for it, not rushing, closing the distance between him and Harry - then throwing another right cross.

The punch connected with the side of Harry's neck, driving him sideways. He let go the knife. When Harry hit the floor, the darkness seemed to vibrate, and Charlie knew it was over. He sagged. Felt his thoughts lose focus. Heard Harry's ragged breathing – the sound like a blowtorch – but as from a great distance.

"Dennis," he whispered. He exhaled so deeply it felt like death. Pain and exhaustion gripped him. He tried to wipe the sweat from his eyes. Then the world spun away from him.

# THIRTY-NINE

December 20<sup>th</sup>. Manor Comprehensive was dark and cold. It smelled of cabbage, disinfectant, and piss. The school had seemed enormous when he was a kid. Now it felt as if the corridor leading to the Biology labs had been shrunk to fit him. Charlie ran a few paces. Then turned to look over his shoulder. All he could see was darkness, thick as a winter blanket. Yet he knew the Tombs' brothers were close by.

He tried the first of the labs, but it was locked. He tried another door and another. These too were locked, and the sound of footsteps grew closer, closer. Blindly, he pushed against another door, and this one swung suddenly open.

It felt like the darkness was sucking him inwards. The sound of his feet on the stone floor came at him. Here the smell of piss was stronger than out on the corridor. Starlight from a tiny window high on the far wall illuminated the urinals, white as bone. Charlie could reach the window, but he knew he'd never be able to squeeze through it. There was only one way out...

But when Charlie turned from the window, Alan, Michael, Daniel and Aden Tombs faced him, their skeletal features picked out by the pale light.

"We owe you," Alan Tombs said and, reaching inside his coat, drew out the bayonet.

"You're dead," Charlie said - a statement not a threat. At which point Dennis stepped from the darkness to stand beside the Tombs brothers.

"He's dead, I'm dead, but debts still have to be paid," Dennis said, his voice a cruel whisper.

"I don't owe you anything."

"You could have saved me, Charlie."

"No." Charlie shook his head emphatically, his tongue working at the dryness inside his mouth.

"Sure you could," Dennis insisted, "but you wanted to steal my wife – so you let me die. And now -"

But as they advanced on him, Charlie escaped the dream, coming awake suddenly.

Sodium light leaked through the curtains just as it had the night two years ago when Dennis was killed. It'd been two years since Dennis's death. Two years since Rachel returned the stolen money to the building society, citing an emotional breakdown as the cause of such an irrational act. Two years since he told her what really happened with the Tombs brothers. Two years…

Charlie waited for his heartbeat to slow, for the pain in his left wrist to subside before he turned to look at Rachel. She was still sleeping and the sight of her comforted him, but, wide-awake now, he eased from the bed, dressed in a tracksuit, and padded downstairs.

It was warm out, the streets sweaty. Even so Charlie ran slowly at first, letting his muscles loosen. Then he picked up the pace, working hard, though not too hard, for the interview was at 2PM and he didn't want to look worn out.

FORTY

In black trousers and a green funnel-necked pullover, Rachel Grant crossed the room to stand beside Charlie.

"I'm nervous," she admitted.

"Me too."

They left the house at exactly 1.30PM.

Coal black clouds pressed down on the rooftops, but the rain held off. They parked where a school used to be and walked the length of Matthew Road to reach the offices of Social Services.

Inside it was too warm – a cloying, claustrophobic heat. In the waiting area Charlie sat self-consciously trying not to look self-conscious. Rachel plucked a magazine from the glass-topped table before them, but before she could open it they were summoned over an intercom into Interview Room 4.

The room was small and rectangular. Something flowery had been sprayed to mask the smell of cigarette smoke. A woman, tall, her right nostril pierced, stood to greet them.

"I'm Katherine Baker," Katherine Baker said.

Charlie and Rachel Grant introduced themselves then were invited to sit before Katherine Baker's desk.

"This meeting is really just to confirm some details," Katherine Baker said, and proceeded to work her way through the form they'd submitted: confirming their full names, their address, their ages, that they'd been married eighteen months.

"What made you leave the police force Mr Grant?"

Charlie had known she'd ask and still the answer came hard.

"My brother was a policeman. He was killed. I reached a..." He shrugged. "...A breakpoint..." He turned to Rachel. Her smile comforted him. "Now I'm a security consultant."

The interview continued, then, until Katherine Baker said:

"Thank you." She sat back. "These details will be put on our database. Then you wait. When - if - a child becomes available, we'll contact you."

Afterwards, they sat drinking coffee at a café in the Benbury town centre indoor market. The lines in Rachel's face were deeper than they had been two years ago, but because they were lines of strength not weakness, Charlie found them easy to be around. The aroma of bacon wafted past them. It smelled good, but he had no appetite. His eyes were tired. He was glad it was over.

"We're okay," Rachel said.

"I know," he said, and reached across the table to clothe her hand with his. "I know," Charlie repeated, suddenly close to tears.